THE CHOKED CASTLE

The Choked Castle

Chris Beech

Contents

Published by Thuo Books 2025

If discovered in the Royal Privy
please return to:

1

The arrival

S hadowed by the forest, the carriage drew to a halt and two figures slipped out. They darted from tree to tree, aware that they might be observed from the castle battlements. Beatrice's heartbeat crescendoed until it almost deafened her. A stitch stabbed into her side and she tugged at her father Peter's sleeve to let her snatch a moment's breath.

Within minutes, they were wading through the grassy moat rippling with sky blue love-in-a-mists and forget-me-nots. The face of Great Roseindid Castle was choked with ivy, which was clawing its way around the remaining stone walls. Chains of it clung to the frame of the servants' entrance, through which they stormed the castle.

"Oh Cook," Peter laughed, giving her a hug. "I see Father's still not worried about invasion. This castle is no more protected than a villager's cottage."

"No indeed, Prince Peter, but then I'm ready with my rolling pin if any invasion force, other than you, should choose to come through the kitchen!"

The kitchen door swung open and a girl, a year older than Beatrice, appeared. Her eyes shone with delight to see the young Princess who she had played with so often during their childhood.

"Molly!" exclaimed Peter, "You've turned into a young woman over the winter and such a pretty one. How are you and your mother keeping? Hope Cook isn't too much of a battle-axe!"

Before Molly had a chance to answer, Cook brandished the rolling pin playfully and Peter and Beatrice slipped away laughing into the corridor.

As they entered the Great Hall, with the newly-finished Peace Tapestry covering one of the its walls, they could hear the sound of Peter's youngest sister Isabel singing from the nearby Hall. Her voice was so beautiful, as clear and pure as a mountain stream cascading over rocks, that they stopped still for a few minutes, immersed in the moment.

As they were listening, a young woman, her face framed with dark curls, came into the Great Hall. Intent on arranging a bowl of roses, she did not notice them for a few moments.

"Auntie Clemence!"Beatrice exploded in delight, running towards her with her arms spread wide. She loved all her aunts but, through the years, Clemence had been the one to touch her heart most. Always generous with her time and able to enter Beatrice's imaginary world with her, Clemence had been her best friend as well as her auntie.

Clemence enveloped Beatrice in her arms and smiled at Peter, until both her cheeks were crowned with dimples. They were soon interrupted by a higher pitched voice.

"Peter, Beatrice! How long have you been here? Why on earth didn't you let the rest of us know, Clemence? You know that I've been watching out all morning from the battlements. Just like you to hog them! Isabel, stop your singing for a minute! They've arrived and we didn't even know, at least most of us didn't."Helen gave a final glare at Clemence, who by now was scarlet-cheeked and ready to excuse herself to avoid further embarrassment. Peter put a reassuring arm round her shoulders.

"No need to fuss, Helen. We only arrived a few moments before you found us. Poor old Clemence didn't have time to call you."

A smaller version of Helen appeared at the door. The same fair complexion and auburn hair. However, Isabel had curls like Clemence, whereas Helen's hair was straight and pulled back into a thick plait. Isabel wore a yellow silk gown. Her smile radiated so much joy and her singing voice was so powerful that they seemed almost disproportionate with her petite stature. The rest of the family were all tall but Isabel had been born prematurely and had never quite caught up. However, she liked being the baby of the family.

Daintily, Isabel darted forward and kissed them both on each cheek.

"Come on you two," she insisted, "You've just got to see your new quilts. I spent all winter stitching them, with some help from Mother. I can't wait to see your faces."

Swinging open the door, Isabel led the way up the staircase, past the ornately carved panels of entwined roses. Helen bounded up the stairs behind them. Clemence set off to find her parents, to let them know of the arrival. She knew that she would find them in the Solar, since both King Geoffrey and Queen Matilda enjoyed escaping royal formalities by coming to this family room adjoining their chamber.

2

The need for a tutor

"Oh Isabel, I can't believe there are so many. They're all gorgeous!"Beatrice gasped.

All the Princesses were gathered together in the Bower adjoining the Queen's chamber. Beatrice sat down on the oak chest next to Clemence. Isabel had just flung open the chests containing all the gowns for them to plan what they were going to wear the following evening. This was to be Beatrice's first court dance at the castle, as these were usually only held in the winter and she had been too young to attend the previous one.

However, this was a special Midsummer court dance to welcome her aunts' new tutor, who was coming highly recommended from the neighbouring kingdom of Renetia.

Isabel pulled out a golden gown, which glowed in the dimly-lit room. This had been hers last winter and, without the fur-trimmed cape that went with it, it would be perfectly suitable for summer. Helen found a turquoise silk gown, from the Midsummer court dance held three years previously, when she was just sixteen.

Clemence was more hesitant than her sisters. After a few minutes of twiddling her dark curls round her index finger, she gave a sigh.

"Come on Beatrice. Let's get you sorted out next."

Isabel foraged through the dresses and pulled out a beautiful pink silk dress with rose buds embroidered over the bodice.

5

"This is sure to fit. It's what I wore to the last Midsummer court dance, when I was about your age and back then it was rather too big for me. Isn't it pretty? It was my favourite gown for a long time."

Smiling, with her hazel eyes sparkling in the firelight, Isabel handed the dress to Beatrice. Then she turned her gaze on Clemence.

"Come on Clemence, what are you going to wear?"

"I'm not really sure. I don't think I've got any best summer gowns that will fit any more. I certainly can't wear the one I wore then. I was only twelve. Maybe I should talk to Mother about it."

"Oh come on Clemence, surely you're not after another new gown? Mother had to get you a new winter one last season because you'd grown," exclaimed Helen.

Blushing deeply, Clemence explained that she was going to ask if she could borrow one of her mother's gowns, as there would not be time for a new one to be made anyway.

Beatrice snuggled a little closer to Clemence and, when the others had left to try on their gowns, quietly rested her head against her shoulder and whispered earnestly,

"You can have the pink one if you like. I'm sure you'd look beautiful in it."

Clemence gave her a hug and replied,

"Thank you Beatrice, that was very generous of you. The pink gown is your special dress now and I can't wait to see you wearing it. I'm sure Mother will find me something suitable to wear."

Queen Matilda did not keep her daughter waiting long. By evening she had produced an emerald silk gown with gold embroidered sleeves.

"It was my favourite dress from when I was the young queen here. You've got my dark hair dear, so the colouring should suit you just as well."

She gave Clemence a little smile and placed the gown in her hands. Then the Queen gave each of her daughters and Beatrice a necklace to suit their gowns. Helen had a sapphire blue one, Clemence's was of emeralds, Isabel's one was of fire opals and Beatrice's of pearls.

King Geoffrey and Peter joined them in the Solar as they were all trying their necklaces on.

"Oh Mother, Peter quipped. "You just don't love me as much as the others! No new jewellry to match my party attire, I see."

"Never mind my boy," King Geoffrey boomed, "I'll search you out a pair of my old embroidered gloves if it'll make you feel special."

"Oh yes, please Father," Peter responded, fluttering his eyelashes. "I do so want to make a good impression on old Osne, the terribly talented tutor."At this all three sisters turned on him.

"You know full well that he's called Aaron Xavier Osne and actually he does sound rather talented doesn't he, unlike some men that I know. Apparently he is an accomplished dance master and singing tutor as well."

Helen's hazel eyes rested reproachfully on her brother.

"I do hope that he is as talented as his extraordinarily high recommendation suggested," Queen Matilda mused. "The mystery is why they ever let him go. There are so many new dances to learn that I am sure that the Renetian royal family could have continued to benefit from his inspired tuition."

"Oh Mother, don't go on so," interrupted Isabel, "I'm sure he's just as wonderful as his reputation. Besides, anyone's got to be better than Priscilla!"

Everyone laughed at that, except Beatrice, who asked,
"Who's Priscilla?"

"Priscilla was our governess when we were little," explained Helen. "She was very kind but when it came to the finer things of life she had two left feet and was completely tone deaf. That's why Mother taught us how to dance and gave us singing lessons in the evenings."

"But there is only so much that a mother can teach her girls," explained Queen Matilda, "and with the wonderful voice you have Isabel, it would be wrong not to help your talent to flourish."

3

Striking a chord

Beatrice smoothed down the folds of her gown, checked that her necklace was hanging evenly and took one final deep breath, before plunging into the cascade of people. The court dance was noisier, brighter and more exciting than she could have imagined. Swirling skirts of jade, crimson and saffron rustled past her in sweeping brush strokes. She found herself instinctively backing herself up against the wood-panelled wall so that she could absorb the scene before she joined in herself.

Suddenly a pair of wide duck's bill shoes appeared in front of her and a hand bedecked with a richly embroidered glove reached out to her.

"Your Highness, may I have the pleasure of your first dance?"

Hardly daring to look up, Beatrice gave a little giggle when she found herself gazing into the grey eyes of her father. Off they flew, skirting round the edge of the Long Gallery, so that Beatrice could enjoy the dancing whilst studying everyone who was there.

"Is that the new tutor?" she whispered to her father, as they were overtaken by a whirling torrent of dance that looked like a radiant Helen, dancing with a distinguished gentleman with jet black hair and a gleaming smile.

"Yes indeed. Helen certainly seems to be enjoying the evening. When we were young, Father held a lot of court dances and Helen always outshone the rest of us."

After dancing with her father, Beatrice sat next to her grandparents and watched the evening unfold. Although he did not look particularly young, Aaron Xavier Osne certainly had plenty of energy. He took it in turns to dance with each of her aunties, until all of them looked exhausted but he still seemed as energetic as ever.

At one stage, Clemence, with her cheeks flushed and her eyes sparkling, brought him over to introduce him to Beatrice. He gave a little nod but then swiftly turned away without asking her for a dance. Beatrice hoped that Clemence would stay and keep her company for a while but the tutor whispered something in Clemence's ear, she giggled and away they went again, swirling across the dance floor.

Eventually the evening began to draw to a close. Before the guests started to leave, as was customary at the castle at any social gathering, the King announced that his youngest daughter would entertain them with her singing.

Beatrice was surprised to see Isabel's reaction. So many times before, she had seen Isabel step forward to sing, blushing with pride, smiling at her father. This time, however, Isabel glared at the King, her face red with anger and embarrassment. Resentfully, she weaved her way through the visitors. The court musician played an introduction on the keys of the beautifully ornate virginal, which rested on a polished oak table at the end of the room. Once she began, her singing was as beautiful as usual and everyone began to relax. When the song ended, Aaron Xavier Osne stepped forward. Everyone turned in amazement at the interruption.

"Your singing is exquisite but the accompanist does not merit associating himself with your beautiful voice. Allow me. . . "

With that, the tutor strode forward and glared at the court musician until he stood up. Seating himself at the virginal, Aaron started with a much more intricate introduction to the same song and throughout gave a virtuoso performance with his hands gliding effortlessly over the full range of the keyboard. Isabel sang her part again but this time to much more rapturous applause.

Beatrice was puzzled. As far as she was concerned, Isabel's singing had sounded better with the simpler accompaniment. At times it had been quite hard to hear her voice, as the playing was much intricate than before. Still, she was pleased to see how happy Isabel looked. She glanced round to see where Helen and Clemence were. Helen was protesting loudly to the King that the evening should end with a dance since, after all, it was court dance not a concert. Clemence was nowhere to be seen.

King Geoffrey conceded, allowing Aaron to whirl Helen around the Long Gallery one final time. Beatrice nestled against her father. He would be leaving the next morning, going back to govern the eastern part of the kingdom for King Geoffrey. This had happened every summer, further back than she could remember, since her mother, Katherine had died giving birth to her. She always missed her father but her aunties had, without fail, kept her busy and happy through the summer months. She had nothing to worry about.

4

Summoned by a letter

The next two weeks felt strange and Beatrice was unsure how to fill her days. For the first time during one of her summers at Great Roseindid Castle, she felt lonely. Previously she had struggled to find a moment on her own to write to her father. Her aunties had spent many hours a day between them sharing their treasured hobbies with her. This year seemed different though. Even when she was with them, her aunts seemed to be distracted.

This morning, Beatrice had gone up to the Council Chamber, in search of Clemence. She had heard that in Great Grandfather Peter's day, this had been an important state room. However, King Geoffrey preferred to welcome his visitors to the Great Hall and allowed his children to use the Council Chamber as a games room.

Beatrice was relieved to see Clemence sitting at the oak games table, where the two of them had spent many happy hours playing the board game, Fox & Geese. She had always loved playing in this room, with its shiny coat of arms on a shield and jewel-handled swords crossed behind it, as a centre-piece opposite the hearth. The flickering firelight was reflected by the jewels, sending beams of ruby light dancing jubilantly across the room.

However, as she approached, she noticed that Aaron was sitting opposite Clemence and that they were playing chess. Their heads were leaning forward, so that they were almost touching. As Beatrice drew closer, she was upset that Clemence did not even acknowledge her presence. She was unsure that Clemence had even noticed her. It seemed that Clemence's world had reduced to the size of the games table and Aaron. Suddenly the silence was broken by Aaron's melodious voice,

"I'm so sorry, my dear Princess Clemence, but I think you'll find that it is 'Check mate' to me!"

"That's not fair!"interrupted Beatrice."You didn't warn her by saying 'Check' last time. She should win the game, not you."

Aaron's brow furrowed in disdain.

"I don't believe that any such rule exists where I come from. However, I'm loath to let my reputation be tarnished by such an accusation."

Clemence was now crimson with shame.

"Oh Beatrice, how could you say such a thing? I would have lost the game anyway, no amount of warnings could have saved me. Aaron is simply a wonderful player."

Stumbling backwards, with her head bowed between her arched shoulders, Beatrice fled from the Council Chamber and ran down the stairs. She wished more than anything else that her father was there to envelope her in one of his hugs. She slipped into the Great Hall to be alone. However, Molly was already in there, down on her hands and knees cleaning out the hearth.

"I'm sorry Princess Beatrice, I didn't realise anyone would want to be in here at this time of day. Would you like me to leave?"

However, when Molly saw Beatrice's face crumpled in distress, where she was trying so hard not to cry, she quickly got to her feet.

"Whatever's wrong, Beatrice? Who could have upset you like this?" Molly asked, her eyes widening with concern. When Beatrice did not answer her but started crying instead, Molly told her gently.

"You just stay here. I'm going to fetch my mum. She'll know what to do."

Presently, Beatrice found herself seated at the kitchen table. Molly's mother Amy was sitting next to her, her arm round Beatrice's shoulders. Looking up at her round, kindly face and greying hair swept back into a neat bun, Beatrice felt reassured. Cook had given her a plate of gingerbread. This had been a favourite of Beatrice's when she was a little girl and Cook always made sure that she had made a batch of it whenever she visited.

"Now Beatrice, if Princess Clemence is so captivated by Mr. Osne, why don't you go and ask Princess Isabel to let you visit the royal menagerie with her. I believe the latest litter of guinea pigs are old enough to be handled now."

Beatrice trusted Amy completely. She had always given good advice in the past. Tossing her golden curls out of her eyes, Beatrice made her way through the castle in search of her youngest auntie. Finding Isabel in the past had never been a problem, since she was always singing, her clear, sweet voice radiating through the castle.

Strangely today though, the castle seemed silent. It was only when Beatrice entered the music chamber, that she found Isabel. With her hands on either side of her waist, she was studiously practising breathing exercises, with Aaron standing in front of her, tapping a steady beat with his fingernails on the table. The sound made Beatrice shudder. Ignoring her presence, Aaron continued the singing lesson.

"You must extend the range of your breathing to develop your singing to its full potential. This will require extensive practice of vocal exercises every day. In the mean time, you must conserve your voice. No more singing around the castle. Only sing when I am present and able to give you proper direction."

Knowing how important singing was to Isabel, Beatrice retreated without saying a word. She was very upset by what she had heard but after her last encounter with Aaron, she felt that there was no point in criticising him in front of her aunties.

It irritated Beatrice that, even at dinner, Aaron was the centre of everyone's attention. He was placed in Peter's usual seat, between Helen and King Geoffrey and opposite Beatrice. Although Beatrice was sitting next to Clemence, she barely got to speak to her, as Clemence, like the other aunties, was entirely focused round the whims and wishes of Aaron. King Geoffrey tried to humour Beatrice with tales of when he was a shy and rather clumsy prince, so different from his heroic older brothers. Normally everyone would have been laughing at these tales. Today, however, Beatrice was the only one listening to him and she struggled to smile at the right places.

Beatrice was surprised to see Molly sheepishly appear at the door of the Great Hall. Normally, the servants only interrupted them here to serve food. However, Molly had a letter clasped in her hand. Going up quietly behind Aaron, she said in a voice barely above a whisper,

"Excuse me sir, there's a letter here with the Renetian royal seal on it. I was told to deliver it into your hands immediately."

Aaron turned to look at the owner of the gentle voice and took the letter carefully from her.

"Thank you," he replied in his low, charming tone, meeting her eyes with his. Blushing, Molly curtsied and left.

All conversations had ceased around the table and everyone held their breath while he opened the letter. Never had such a private, royal letter been sent to anyone here except King Geoffrey.

Aaron peeled back the wax seal and unfurled the letter. His forehead furrowed in displeasure. Helen leaned a little in towards him, asking who the letter was from.

Swiftly he folded the page down towards him, then folded it exactly in half and then in half again, running his long thumb nail along the creases so that they were sharp and perfectly precise.

"Would you mind explaining what matter of such extreme urgency merited this disturbance?"

Aaron's eyes rose to meet Queen Matilda's and Beatrice saw anger, like a flash of lightning pass across his face. He was not used to being challenged by anyone. Within a few moments though, he had regained his composure.

"I do apologise for this intrusion, your Majesty. However, I am bound by honour not to reveal the contents of this letter. Suffice it to say that it involves a matter of life and death. In view of what I have read, my presence and skills are needed urgently. I humbly request permission to leave for Renetia at once. I apologise profusely for the inconvenience this will cause you and promise to return for the start of my official duties as tutor here from the first day of September."

"Of course, dear fellow," King Geoffrey replied kindly. "You may travel in the royal carriage."

5

———

Return to happiness

Beatrice smiled to herself as she watched the carriage pull away towards the stormy sky. She noticed that Queen Matilda also kept calm throughout the farewells, unlike her distraught daughters. Isabel declared that she would not sing a single note until he returned. Helen packed away her dancing shoes and informed the Queen that her best satin slippers were so wore that they would need replacing before his return. She suggested that purchasing white satin slippers embroidered with pearls might console her in her distress. The Queen just snorted.

Beatrice noticed that Clemence had disappeared. After searching the Long Gallery and the Council Chamber, she bumped into Molly.

"Have you seen Clemence, Molly?"

Molly hesitated for a moment, biting her lip.

"I'm not allowed to say anything but if I was looking for a missing friend, I'd try listening outside their chamber."

With her ear pressed to the solid oak door, Beatrice could just make out the sound of sobbing. She could wait no longer. She burst into the chamber and threw her arms around Clemence's trembling form.

<div align="center">~~~~~~~~~~</div>

After a week of thundery showers, the fine weather returned and so did her aunties' good humour. Isabel's singing echoed around the castle, as she practised the songs that she been learning with Aaron.

Each morning, after breakfast, Isabel took Beatrice to see the guinea pig pups, one black, one brown and two white but with the smaller of the two having pronounced black markings to one side of her eye and pale pink ears. Isabel and Beatrice both loved cuddling the pups nestled in the palm of their hands, with their feet so huge in comparison to the rest of their bodies. The aunties had named a guinea pig each but the little white one they had left for Beatrice to name.

"Cleo," Beatrice declared, gazing at the tiny guinea pig cradled warmly in her hand."Definitely a Cleo."

Each day, after dinner, Helen took Beatrice for a walk round the royal palace gardens. She pointed out a swan's nest and the small gap in the hedge where rabbits squeezed their way through to feast on the royal carrots and turnips. They played tennis and practised archery together. Sometimes, when she was in a good mood, she even allowed Beatrice to ride her own beautiful chestnut mare Serenity, instead of the little pony Smudge.

Beatrice's favourite time of day though was the evening. This was when Clemence curled up on her four-poster bed with her and read her the stories she had written, many of them especially for Beatrice. They were full of princesses with blonde curly hair, suspiciously like Beatrice's, who had adventures with gallant guinea pigs and heroic horses! Clemence had made up stories for her every year, as far back as she could remember. Sometimes she had even stitched little dolly versions of the characters whilst Beatrice was asleep, so that she woke from her pleasant dreams to find the princess and her friends beside her on the pillow.

By the last day of her holiday, Beatrice could tell that the summer was over. The mornings were colder and swathed with mist. Darkness came sooner every evening. It was time to go home. By the time that her father came to collect her, Beatrice's tale of her holiday was full of nothing but happy memories, as it had always had been.

However, as they were leaving the castle grounds, a shadowy figure passed them on horseback. The slender figure and flowing black hair made him instantly recognisable.

"Surely that was the tutor fellow. Whatever possesses him to gallop at that speed? Surely even Isabel isn't in need of an emergency singing lesson!" Peter quipped. Not wanting to dwell further on this topic, Beatrice quickly started to tell her father about the baby guinea pigs.

6

New Year's Eve

Back at her home, Gorsebank Castle, Beatrice felt very lonely. What made it worse was the rain pounding against the leaded glass window in her chamber, even more monotonously than usual. In the past, Clemence's letters, which were often accompanied with stories or illustrations, had proved a powerful remedy to the loneliness she felt on returning home. Disappearing off to her chamber, she would curl up in the window seat, cuddling a selection of the dolls made for her by Clemence. In the quiet room, she could almost hear Clemence's soft, gentle voice speaking to her through these letters.

Queen Matilda also wrote to her regularly, in her elegant script and embossed with the royal seal. Her letters were more like a diary of everyday events, told simply. They almost made her feel as if she was still among them, sharing their lives. Helen wrote to Peter, as being closest in age, they had always played together as children. The letters between these two were shorter and full of funny incidents that they wanted to share with each other.

Each year, at the beginning of November, Clemence would write and ask Beatrice what her favourite animals and hobbies were at the moment. Beatrice knew that Clemence would use her answers to write a special story to make up into a New Year book gift for her, with accompanying toy characters. As far as she was aware, this had happened every year of her life and she had a special carved chest for all the books and toys from Clemence to live in. This year she had been thinking of her answers in advance and decided that she would like a book about horses most of all.

However, time crept forward, the letters from Clemence grew shorter and there were no questions about such things. Recently there had been no stories from her either and the only illustrations looked suspiciously like attempts to draw a portrait of Aaron. Beatrice buried these at the bottom of her chest.

New Year's Eve came laden with snow and the carriage bringing presents from the castle only just arrived ahead of a further snowstorm. It was overflowing with gifts as usual, mostly for Beatrice. However, it became clear that all the presents were from her grandparents. There was a new crimson gown, an ivory-white muff and cape trimmed with emerald green and gold embroidery and a jewellry chest, which was a miniature version of the beautiful oak chest at Great Roseindid Castle, with its carved pattern of roses.

Isabel had never had such lavish presents before. However, as she opened the last one, her heart sank that there was no book from Clemence, nor any of the other usual embroidered gifts from her aunties. Unable to suppress the tears welling in her eyes, Beatrice blurted out,

"Oh Father, these are all lovely but it doesn't feel the same without my book from Auntie Clemence."

Peter was silent for a few moments. Then he playfully ruffled her hair."

"I expect they've noticed that you're growing into a fine young lady now, not a little girl any more. They probably just thought these presents would be more suitable. There are some letters though. Shall we have a look?"

Firstly they opened the sealed letter, which was from Queen Matilda. It was reassuring to see the characteristically long letter with a cheerful message added by King Geoffrey. However, when Peter read out the letter from his mother, they were both surprised at the lack of news about the Princesses and that there was barely a word about how they were getting on with their new tutor.

"That's strange," Peter muttered, as he sifted through the letters," Helen normally writes at length at New Year, all about their Christmas entertainments. See what Clemence has to say, will you Beatrice? She's so fond of you, she will surely have written you a good letter."He handed her the letter with a confident smile. Beatrice gingerly unfolded it, hoping for some news, maybe even a story.

Although there was no story, Clemence had written her a short message, explaining that she had been very busy, too busy to ponder over children's stories or to do any sewing. Peter gave Beatrice a hug.

"That's not like Clemence either. She's the kindest person I know. She's always doing something for someone else, especially you."

Peter tore open the letter from Isabel. It was intricately decorated, with a long message inside. Peter drew up a seat and stroked Beatrice's head whilst he read the message aloud.

"My dear Peter and Beatrice,

Time seems to be galloping past these days and I cannot wait for it to arrive at the New Year celebrations. I'm going to sing a duet with Aaron. With a lot of hard work and exercise, he's managed to stretch my range far wider than before, so it should be wonderful.

It will also be such a treat to sing a proper song again, as we spend hours a day perfecting my breathing and tone at the moment. Aaron's such a perfectionist but then he's just perfect and that's what he wants me to be. "

At this point Peter gave a snort, which he tried to turn into a cough for Beatrice's benefit, before continuing to read,

"I'm working so hard at my singing that I don't have much time to rest during the day and sometimes I barely have time to join the family for meals. As you'll appreciate, I have been too busy to sew presents for anyone this year. I'm sure you understand. My present to you all will be my

much improved singing voice. I really don't know how you used to enjoy my old singing so much. Aaron says he's turning a crow into a nightingale. "

Beatrice noticed that her father was holding the letter so tightly that his knuckles were turning white.

"I don't know what's got into Helen. She just dances around all day getting in everyone's way. She keeps interrupting our singing lessons and insisting that Aaron run through the complicated dance steps he's been teaching her. I don't know how he has patience with anyone so slow. I suppose she may be getting tired, as she stays up so late to practise, but it's no excuse really.

Still, Helen's not as bad as Clemence. She's becoming so selfish these days. She hardly bothers to turn up for anything, even banquets. During the last state visit, she locked herself in her chamber and refused to come down. The only person she really talks to is Aaron and then it's all about her poetry and her paintings. He spends plenty of time tutoring her and she's always busy at something but she never lets us see or hear any of her work anymore. Since Aaron pointed out how poorly she had painted the family portrait that used to hang in the Council Chamber, she does not think that any of her work is fit to look at.

Anyway, I must stop now and get back to my singing exercises.
Your affectionate sister and auntie, Isabel. "

Peter tossed the letter onto the table.

"Couldn't we go and see them for New Year, Father," Beatrice pleaded. "I miss them all so very much and I'm worried about them."

"So am I" said Peter grimly. "I'd dearly like to have a few words with that so-called tutor and talk some sense into my little sisters. This would have been the last chance we'll get to visit before the summer, because of all my royal duties. However, the weather has been so bad that crossing the River Tovil would be too dangerous. We'd never get through on horseback, let alone in a carriage. I didn't even let Sam attempt the journey back with Father's royal carriage. He'll have to wait for the thaw. "

7

At the end of the twine

On New Year's morning, despite the bitter cold, Beatrice threw back her quilt and ran to her father's chamber. Her face was flushed with excitement. She had the presents that she had secretly been making for him tucked under her shawl.

Not seeing the usual pile of presents near her father, Beatrice decided that she would go first. She pulled out a tiny present from the folds of her shawl. It was a handkerchief that she had embroidered with the royal crest of two dragons intertwined around a shield with a rose on it. It had taken her hours to finish all the tiny stitches, trying so hard to keep the back as neat as the front. Her second present was a scarf, which she had knitted for him in crimson, his favourite colour. She had not been knitting long and one end of the scarf seemed to be rather wider than the other, but her father loved it and immediately wrapped it round his neck.

"It's perfect, Beatrice - and exactly what I need in this cold weather. "

Then, scratching his head and furrowing his brow, Peter continued,

"Now, where did I put your present? I've got a feeling that it's at the other end of this piece of twine. With that, he handed her a length of red twine that had been tucked under his pillow, giving her one of his mischievous smiles.

Clutching the end of the twine, Beatrice followed the red strand under the bed and round the back of the chest. Then, as she followed its path upwards, she realised that it was secured high on the wall as it passed through the doorway. With Peter following closely behind her, Beatrice ran down the stairs and through the Great Hall, with still no end in sight and a huge tangle of twine gathered in her arms. Finally, she ended up in the courtyard, with the trail leading to the great barn.

As their eyes grew accustomed to the darkness, Beatrice spotted a foal standing shyly in the far corner. Its chestnut coat reflected the little light that there was, as daylight was creeping into the barn. It whinnied gently as Beatrice patted its neck.

"She's gorgeous Father, thank you," she managed to say, almost too choked with excitement to speak.

"You realise that it will be a long while before she's big enough to ride but in the meantime you. .."

At this point, Peter was interrupted by a tiny mewing sound. Surprised, Beatrice looked down. Standing behind the foal's front hooves was a little tortoiseshell kitten with white bib and mittens. Beatrice instinctively knelt down in the hay and reached her hands out to the kitten.

"This little one lost her mother when she only a few weeks old. Since then she's been reared in the barn where your foal was raised. When we tried to take the foal, the kitten kept mewing and following after us. Her owner was pleased for us to take charge of the kitten as well, since the two animals are inseparable. The only condition is that you take on the responsibility for hand-rearing her, Beatrice, as she's not yet old enough to fend for herself."

Beatrice nodded excitedly, though most of her attention was drawn to the rhythmic purring that seemed to be welling up inside the kitten.

"You're going to be busy for a while, Beatrice. First of all you need to decide what to call them both. "

For a few moments, Beatrice could not think what to say. Then she decided.

"The foal is called Bright and the kitten Mabel. "

Holding the tiny kitten in cupped hands near her face, she gently asked her if 'Mabel' would be acceptable. There was a loud, affirming purr. Peter burst out laughing.

"I'm surprised you asked the kitten and not the mare," he teased.

"Oh, Father. You only need to look at them to see who is in charge!"

Over the next few weeks, it was shown that Beatrice was an excellent judge of character. Whilst the foal remained gentle and obedient, the kitten grew in confidence and mischief. She would often hide in the manger of hay, springing out to surprise Beatrice. Bright even allowed her to swing on her long, swishing tail, which to the kitten was irresistible.

After her lessons each day, Beatrice would always be found in the stable, chattering away as she coaxed the kitten to lap milk from a saucer and groomed Bright. Time filled with so much joyful labour passed swiftly and she hardly noticed winter passing into spring and the trees crowned in blossom.

8

A visit by night

Peter was glad that Beatrice was so happily occupied, since there had been no letters recently from Great Roseindid Castle and he did not want her to have to share in his anxiety. One evening, long after Beatrice had gone to bed, he was very relieved to see that a messenger had come from the castle.

"Nothing from the Princesses, Sam?"he enquired of the messenger boy, who was being treated to ale and cake after his long ride. Sam, usually so full of chatter, just shook his head and looked down at his boots.

Frowning slightly, Peter hastily opened the letter from his mother. He was shocked at the untidy handwriting. Surely, after all this time, someone could have taken the trouble to write a proper letter to him.

"My dear Peter,

I have little time to write this and I have little to say that I want to be having to say to anyone. However, the situation has grown so far out of my control that I am afraid. I hardly know where to begin.

There seems little peace left in the castle. It feels as if a plague of unhappiness has swept through the very core of our home and the Princesses are rapidly wilting away. Our royal physician is perplexed. No one seems to be suffering from any known illness and yet there is little doubt that all three are ill. However, no matter how ill they seem to us, none of them will be treated as such. In fact, they become angry if we suggest rest or nourishment. Nor will they let me speak of their problems, even inside the castle and they refuse to see the royal physician again, since he recommended the use of leeches. The only reason that I am able to write this letter is that they have all accompanied their tutor to the theatre.

Please do not answer this letter, as they will be very distressed if they think that I have told you about the situation. However, I feel that I should warn you of what is happening so that you can decide for yourself where Beatrice should spend the summer. Please send her our fondest love.

Your ever-loving Mother"

Astonished, Peter turned to Sam

"I hear that there is some ill health in the castle. Do you know anything of this matter?"

Flushed, Sam stumbled over his words,

"It's breaking my heart, your Highness. Molly is fading away before my very eyes. She's always been a dainty little thing but now she's wasting away. Amy has to carry the coal scuttle for her and she fainted clean away yesterday when she tried to climb up to dust the top of the fireplace."

"That's distressing news Sam. I'm so sorry. I know you've always been fond of Molly. Have you heard of any other cases of Molly's problem in the castle?"

Sam looked down and slowly shook his head.

"I'd best be going, your Highness. Thank you for your kind words and for the cakes."

With that, Sam set off into the night, with Peter absentmindedly watching until he had finally disappeared. He was unsure whether he should mention anything about the letter to Beatrice.

Peter sat by the fire, reading and re-reading it, wondering what he should do for the best. He wished so much that his beloved Katherine were still alive to advise him. Emptiness consumed him and he became lost in thought until the early hours. As he climbed slowly up the stairs to his chamber, he noticed Beatrice's door ajar. He wondered if she had heard Sam's arrival and been waiting for the latest news from the castle.

Softly, Peter pushed the door a little until could see Beatrice's sleeping head peacefully settled on the pillow, with the kitten snuggled in the curl of her plait. He smiled to himself, thinking that she would have had Bright tucked up in bed with her too, if she could have got up her up the spiral stairs.

9

The Messenger

As the evenings lengthened, Beatrice became more and more excited about the prospect of going back to Great Roseindid Castle. However, she also began to have nightmares. She would wake up in a cold sweat, calling Clemence's name. On waking, she could not remember the details of the nightmares but they left her feeling anxious.

Beatrice had started going to bed early, as her nights had become so restless. So, when the sound of approaching hooves woke her, she thought at first that it was morning but soon realised that the sun had barely set. In the dim, dusky light she could make out the shape of a rider entering the grounds at full gallop. Immediately she was wide awake.

Pulling back the quilt, she wrapped a shawl around her shoulders and ran down barefoot to meet her father and find out what the matter was. Her feet darted over the cold stone steps swiftly catching up with her father, who had lingered long enough to put on his boots before hastening down to meet the messenger.

Recognising the black stallion as from King Geoffrey's stables, both Peter and Beatrice were expecting to see Sam. However, the figure that had stepped down wearily from the saddle was that of an older man, wrapped in a dark grey riding cape. As he approached them, he flung back his hood.

"Father!" exclaimed Peter.

"Grandad, what's wrong?"Beatrice cried out, unable to contain herself any longer.

Catching his breath, King Geoffrey choked out,

"Peter, we need your help right away. You'll never believe what's been happening."

"Father, you look exhausted, why on earth didn't you send Sam with a message?"

The King's shoulders slumped at this remark and he made no reply.

Beatrice suddenly knew what to do. Grasping him firmly by the arm, she led him through to the Solar, where the embers were still warm.

"Come on Grandad, please sit down and rest."

King Geoffrey collapsed gratefully into one of the stately chairs and gave a weak smile in her direction, as she placed a tapestry-covered footstool under his weary legs.

"Peter, I just don't know what to do. Tell me what to do."

"Hold on, Father. Just take a deep breath and tell me exactly what's been happening to the girls."

"There's so much wrong, it's hard to know where to start. With Isabel, I suppose. She refuses to eat with us at all and only seems to nibble at food, like a bird, says Cook, but it's not really enough to keep a sparrow fed. I don't know if she told you that she was going to sing in a concert at New Year. Well, even by then, she was wearing the dress that she had lent Beatrice. She'd been practising for months but when it came to her duet, her voice was so weak that you couldn't hear her sing. She still spends all day long practising vocal exercises, with a regimented routine. We hear the same few notes being sung over and over, hour after hour, day after day. To be honest, her beautiful voice is gone. She sounds more like an old crow squawking…."

At this the King bent forward, his shoulders hunched in misery.

"Father," said Peter, shocked, "You didn't mention to her anything about being like a crow did you?"

"Certainly not, my boy. Not that she would have believed me if I had. That wretched tutor is the only person she listens to nowadays and he's convinced her that she must keep up this regime, so that her singing can be perfect. We simply can't understand why she believes him. Not only is she not interested in us or our opinions any more, Isabel has also stopped caring for the animals in the menagerie. We realised after a while that the poor little creatures weren't being taken care of at all. She'd even stopped giving them fresh food and water. Your Mother wouldn't put up with this any longer. Only yesterday, she told Isabel that no one else in the castle was going to starve and that the animals must be given to the village children to care for, with us providing sufficient funds for their upkeep."

At this, Beatrice blurted out,

"Grandad, what do you mean? Who at the castle has starved? Please tell me?"

Both King Geoffrey and Peter were startled at her voice. Both had forgotten her for a moment.

"Don't worry, my dear Beatrice. All your aunties will soon be better. I just need you and your father to come back with me tomorrow morning, that's all."

"Yes, Beatrice, and because we will need to make an early start and do lots of packing first, I suggest that you should hurry off to bed now and get as much sleep fitted into the remaining hours of tonight as possible. To be honest, father, you look as if you need a rest too. You can tell us the rest of the news as we are travelling together in the carriage tomorrow."

Although Beatrice felt frustrated and terribly worried by what she had heard, she could scarcely keep her eyes open. Alone in her chamber, she drifted off to sleep, wondering what could have caused so huge a change from the happiness they had shared last summer.

10

The journey home

Having said her goodbyes to Bright and Mabel, Beatrice hurried out to the carriage. She had her shawl tightly pulled around her to keep out the driving rain. The chest of dresses that she had hastily packed for the summer was so full that she could scarcely fasten it.

Beatrice sat facing her Grandad. In the daylight, she could see that his face was far more furrowed than it had been last summer. Despite having had some sleep, dark shadows hung under his eyes, as if some huge burden was still resting on his shoulders.

"Grandad, why didn't you send Sam to pick us up?"

King Geoffrey bit his lip, glancing down to his lap, where his clasped hands seemed to be battling against each other.

"I would rather not have to tell either of you this. However, since you are coming to the castle, I cannot spare you from the pain any longer. Sam was unable to come because he was too distressed. You see, it has not only been the Princesses who have been troubled recently. We didn't really realise how ill Molly had become until it was too late to save her. None of us know why exactly but she seemed to starve herself to death..."

Peter put his arm around Beatrice and she could feel that he was trembling too.

"Father," Peter gasped, "Do you really mean that dear little Molly is dead?"

Without a word, the King nodded, keeping his eyes firmly fixed on his lap.

"I don't understand, Grandad. How could anyone starve at your castle? There is always so much wonderful food there and the servants always have plenty to eat too."

At this, King Geoffrey met her gaze and held out his hands.

"My sweet child, that's the tragedy of it. She just seemed to lose her understanding that she needed to eat to stay alive."

After this, there was a long pause before anyone spoke again. Beatrice was leaning against her father's shoulder, tears welling up silently, even though she was trying to be brave.

"Father, this illness is much more deadly than I had realised. Naturally I will come and help as you requested. However, don't you think Beatrice should stay behind? It seems to strike at young ladies and Beatrice is all I've got left."

Before Beatrice had a chance to answer for herself, King Geoffrey replied,

"My dear boy, don't think that we have forgotten about Beatrice. Her well-being is of the greatest importance to us all. However, since your mother last wrote to you, we have a greater understanding of what has been happening. We now realise that the cause of this illness is an insidious poison, not a disease to be caught."

"Poison!" exclaimed Peter, "Who on earth would want to poison the Princesses and Molly?"

"Can't you guess?" said the King. "It's that highly recommended tutor of theirs. Queen Matilda soon began to dislike him but I saw nothing wrong in him other than an overbearing pride.

However, it appears that his words have been pouring poison into their minds. We have longed on countless occasions to dismiss Aaron Xavier Osne but alas, to no avail. The Princesses will not have a word said against him. They treat us like servants and him like a prince. It perplexes me as to how he charms them so. It is now quite apparent that he is both manipulative and destructive but they are all blind to his faults.

Queen Matilda felt that if you came alone to the castle, Peter, your sisters would be suspicious and immediately defend him. However, if your visit were simply seen as you bringing Beatrice to us for the summer, they should have no objection. They will just see it as another of your innocent games, arriving early as usual so as to surprise us. Besides, consumed in their own thoughts as they are, they are unlikely to notice the date, as each day seems but a grim copy of the previous one."

As the early morning mist unfolded over the sweeping vista of Great Roseindid, both Peter and Beatrice breathed a little more easily. It was a beautiful morning and the air was fresh with dew, stirring the familiar fragrance of the wildflower-strewn meadow, bringing back memories of previous summers here. It was so refreshing to escape from the constant rain in the Eastern Province. Surely the situation at the castle would not be quite as bad as the King's description had led them to believe.

"How is Auntie Clemence? She's not ill like Auntie Isabel is she?"

"And Helen, Father, you've not told us about either of them," Peter prompted.

King Geoffrey, whose anxiety had been growing the closer he got to the castle, looked across the carriage at Peter and answered him first.

"Helen is almost like a hideous exaggeration of herself. As you know, she's always loved taking walks and dancing. Now it is almost impossible to stop her from doing one or other of these activities. It's so continuous that I wake to the sound of her feet dancing along the Gallery and I fall asleep to the same unrelenting sound."

"Surely, if Auntie Helen is dancing, she must be feeling joyful," interrupted Beatrice, hoping to make her Grandad look less unhappy.

"I'm afraid not, Beatrice dear - quite the opposite. She seems more miserable every day, though when we plead with her to stop, that also causes anguish. Often she is practising dance steps with that infernal Aaron. In between dance sessions, he has told her that she must take long walks to get fitter and to improve her dancing skills. No one ever minded her strolling around the grounds for as long as she liked. Nowadays though, she wanders away from the safety of the castle on her own, walking for hours at a time. She seems compelled to go no matter what the weather – rain, blazing sunshine, even thunder and lightning don't stop her. I suppose she does eat more than Isabel but then nothing like as much as she needs. She too has become gaunt, like her sister."

"But Grandad, what about Auntie Clemence?"Beatrice burst out.

"Beatrice, stop these rude interruptions at once! Let your grandfather finish what he was saying!"

Beatrice had never been spoken to in such a harsh, angry tone, whether by her father or anyone else. She went white and started trembling.

"Oh Beatrice, I'm sorry," Peter said, "This situation is a terrible strain for all of us. Could you tell us how Clemence is, Father?"

"Clemence has always done things her own way and this is no different. However, although her symptoms may sound less worrying, that's far from how I feel about the way she has been acting. She has become unrecognisably thin and angry even since that wretched tutor encouraged her to trim her figure for the New Year Ball, so that she did not look out of place with her sisters. Clemence fasts all day and then goes to the kitchen two hours before dinner and starts screaming at Cook about the preparations for the meal. She demands a banquet every day. She eats far more than any man I've ever known, as if she's famished. Then, despite everyone having followed her instructions, she bursts into tears and leaves the Great Hall early. None of the food seems to do her any good. She is as thin and ill-looking as the others. Queen Matilda and I are at our wits' ends trying to make them see sense. We hope that you can m'boy. They've always listened to you."

11

A reunion with unhappiness

"Where have you been?" A sharp voice greeted the King as he entered the castle through the gatehouse. Looking up, Beatrice could see a face that looked a little like her Aunt Helen glaring down on them from the battlements. By the time that they had entered the Great Hall, they heard the thundering of feet descending the stone stairs. As the figure pierced through the doorway, both Peter and Beatrice stepped back in horror.

Helen stood in front of them, her eyes burning with anger and her fists clasped so that her knuckles protruded whitely. Instead of greeting her brother and niece, she turned on her father in fury.

"What have you brought them here for? What good do you think that will do?" she hissed, in a voice that neither Peter or Beatrice would have recognized as Helen's. Without waiting for an answer, Helen fled back up the stairs and they could hear her pounding feet fading into the distance.

Peter had taken hold of Beatrice's hand when Helen started her outburst. He said nothing for a moment but gently squeezed her hand. He had no words to describe his feelings about what he had just seen. Before either had time to compose themselves, a harsh shrill voice screamed out,

"Shut up, out there. You know I'm practising my singing exercises. You've interrupted me and now I'll have to start all over again."

Peter let go of Beatrice's hand and moved swiftly towards the Hall, opening the door and entering it. At first, Isabel ignored the intruder but then, sensing that this was someone different from usual, she spun round to confront them. No one in the castle dared to interrupt her any more. Seeing Peter startled her. For a moment she stood still, looking at him. Peter was shocked by what he saw.

As with Helen, all the life had been drained from Isabel's face and her dress was hanging loosely over her bony frame, held together by a plaited cord. What was so startling in Isabel's case was the loss of her beautiful smile. Her cheeks were so hollowed out, that it was hard to imagine that she could smile any more. He noticed her eyes flickering agitatedly, as if she was trying to work out how to respond to this unforeseen meeting. It looked as if she wanted him to go away but he stood his ground, hoping to see, even for an instant, a glimmer of the Isabel he had always known.

~~~~~~~~~~

Back in the Great Hall, Beatrice was growing impatient to see Clemence. Her father had disappeared to talk to Auntie Isabel. The King had gone to inform Queen Matilda of his return, leaving Beatrice alone. Although she was frightened of meeting Aunt Helen, she decided that it would be worth the risk of going upstairs in the hope of finding Auntie Clemence.

Slipping the wooden pattens off her feet, so that she could climb the stone stairs silently in her silk slippers, Beatrice reached the next floor. She could hear Helen's feet tapping away rhythmically. Thankfully they were retreating further away from her along the Gallery. This must be the dancing that her Grandad had spoken of. She was thankful to reach the Council Chamber without being observed. She slipped in quietly, hoping Clemence might be there, as she had been so often in the past, writing or doing her needlework in this peaceful room.
~~~~~~~~~~

Beatrice froze as she saw Aaron sitting at the far side of the oak games table. Looking more closely at the two seated figures, Beatrice felt a shiver of fear pass through her. Aaron looked spry, vigorous and youthful. This was a stark contrast to the withered figure sitting opposite him, reaching out for a chess piece with a hand that was shaking and almost claw-like.

Beatrice did not want to recognise this person but the winter shawl pulled tightly around the hunched over shoulders was the one that she had given as a special New Year present for Auntie Clemence, having spent many hours embroidering it with holly leaves and berries. Beatrice stood there, too stunned to speak.

"Are you seriously telling me that's the best move you can manage after all that time? You're useless, utterly useless. I don't know why I waste my time on you."

Anger welled up inside Beatrice and she longed to shout at Aaron. However, before she could open her mouth, she remembered the last time that she had watched them play chess and she did not want to repeat that nightmare again, not if she could help it. She watched the scene as her auntie cradled her head in her hands. Aaron swiftly brought the game to check. Wearily, Clemence retreated the king behind a pawn, knowing that her defence could not hold out for long. Within another two moves, Aaron called out imperiously,

"Check mate again! Really, Clemence, I'm getting so bored with your lazy, incompetent play. I might as well be playing against a child. You need to study harder, to improve your poor intelligence and don't indulge yourself with food. You spend far too much time on such matters. How is it that your sisters manage to control themselves, yet you have no self-discipline?"

Without answering, Clemence tried to flee from the room but her knees seemed to buckle beneath her. Clinging her way along the carved wall panels, she managed to get to the further door and slipped away into the dark Gallery. Beatrice planned to wait quietly where she was until Aaron had left, so that she could follow her auntie and comfort her. However, Aaron's voice suddenly cut across her thoughts.

"Oh, little mouse, don't think you haven't been spotted. Come out of the shadows and let's see what the last year has done to you."

Trembling, Beatrice felt impelled to step forward. After all, she was a royal princess and she had no intention of running away from a mere tutor. To her amazement, he had seated himself on the King's throne raised on the higher level of the dais. Aaron's granite grey eyes seemed to whittle away at her, piece by piece, as if she were no more than a block of wood. Then, suddenly his manner changed. His glare turned to a gracious smile. However, this did not reach his eyes. Nevertheless, there was something inescapably charming about him.

12

The missing daughter

Finally, Peter managed to say,

"It's good to see you, Isabel. Beatrice and I have missed you all so much. We couldn't wait to come this year, so we arrived a little early. How have you been faring?"

Isabel's lip began to tremble. For a moment it seemed as if she did not know what to say. When she did, her words startled Peter.

"I'm sorry Peter but I'm extremely busy with my singing exercises. You and Beatrice are so fortunate, just being able to freely go where and when you like. I'm trapped here in this castle and I've got so much I've got to do. No one cares about what I want. It's always just about them and how they feel. Why doesn't anyone care how I feel? Helen and Clemence are constantly disturbing my practice time and now you're here too. Why can't you all just leave me alone!"

Stunned at her words and at the harshness of her tone, Peter simply turned on his heel and walked away. Isabel had never spoken to him like that. For a moment, he thought he could hear stifled sobbing from behind him. However, he suddenly realised that he had no idea of where Beatrice was and felt frightened. The sobbing could wait.

Finding no one in the Great Hall, Peter hastened to his parents' Solar, where he found the King and Queen huddled together, deep in conversation. The King was slumped forward in his chair with his head in his hands.

"Where's Beatrice?" he asked immediately, without greeting his mother.

"Surely she went with you to see Isabel?" King Geoffrey replied wearily.

No, she did not. I left her in your charge. Where is she?" Peter's heart was pounding. Seeing the puzzled, anxious look on his parents' faces, he realised that he needed to take charge of the situation.

Returning to the Great Hall, he looked around him. Where would his daughter have gone? From upstairs he could the drumming of Helen's dancing feet and realised that she might have seen her. Racing up the stairs, he soon reached his sister, swirling her way at high speed along the Gallery.

"Helen, have you seen Beatrice?"

Circling on the spot, but unable to stop the dance, Helen looked at Peter with strange, frightened eyes.

"Oh Peter, why do you ask me? I saw her with you when you both arrived. The only person I've seen since then is Clemence. She bundled past me in an awful state, bumping into me. She was on her way to her chamber."

Having managed to stay in one place this long, Helen whirled away down the Gallery, leaving Peter stunned. He barely recognised his sisters and their behaviour was alien to anything he had known before. He suddenly understood why his elderly father had ridden so fast to fetch him and why he had found it so difficult to speak of the problems. Then his fear for Beatrice brought him back to the present. He was angry with himself. Why should he feel so frightened for his daughter in the home he had always loved and seen as the safest place in the world for her? Surely he was being unduly fearful, yet terror was creeping over him as surely as rising floodwater.

Clemence's chamber was on the far side of the first floor, overlooking the rose garden. Peter strode there as fast as he could, his heartbeat pounding in his ears. At first when he knocked on the door, there was no answer. Then listening for a minute, he could clearly hear sobbing coming from within. Taking a deep breath, he opened the door. He was surprised that the bed was neatly made and that, at first glance, there was no sign of anyone, though the sobbing was louder. Looking more closely, he noticed a bedraggled heap between the chest and the wall. Clemence, with her shawl wrapped over her head, was curled into a tiny ball.

Peter was so shocked that, for a moment, he forgot about his hunt for Beatrice. Kneeling beside her, he carefully brushed back the forlorn curls from her face.

"Oh Clemence, come here!" he exclaimed, coaxing her out of her shell. "Whatever has happened to upset you this much?"

Reaching out his hands to her, Peter gently eased Clemence to her feet and enveloped her in a hug. Trying hard not to show how horrified he was by her appearance, Peter clung on to what was left of his sister. The cold hands and bony frame protruding through tissue-paper skin made her seem unbearably fragile, like a porcelain doll. She seemed to lack all the warmth she once had. No wonder she was wrapped in a winter shawl. In a barely audible voice, she whimpered,

"Peter, I don't know what's wrong with me. I can't think straight any more. I was so useless at chess that I don't know how Aaron put up with me. I'm such a failure Peter, I really am."

Suddenly Peter remembered Beatrice.

"Clemence, did you see Beatrice? I think she may have been looking for you when she disappeared."

A puzzled expression passed over Clemence's face.

"Beatrice, what would she be doing here? In fact, Peter, why are you here? I don't understand. I can't cope."

Again, Clemence's eyes overflowed with tears. Clearly, she had not seen Beatrice. Peter realised that he must leave her and resume his search.

"Clemence, I'm so sorry to leave you like this but I'm sick with worry about Beatrice and I must go and look for her, though I honestly don't know where to begin."

Clemence just nodded sadly and sank onto a nearby chair so wearily, it looked as though she was carrying a heavy burden.

When Peter had left her chamber, he stopped and listened intently, hoping for some clue as to where Beatrice had gone. All he could hear was the distant tapping of Helen's pattens mechanically swirling along the Gallery and the resumed sobbing from Clemence's chamber.

Desperately Peter thought over what Clemence had said. He remembered that she had been playing chess with Aaron. Perhaps Beatrice had reached the Council Chamber after Clemence had left. He ran on legs that suddenly felt as heavy as tree trunks and hurled the heavy oak door open as soon as he arrived.

13

At the edge of a sword

Rising from his seat and standing still for a moment before stepping down from the dais, Aaron approached Beatrice, his grey eyes still fixed on her. In the flickering firelight, Beatrice had the impression that he was swaying gently from side to side. She was frightened yet intrigued by him and felt unable to move from the spot. With a fluid movement, he drew one of the ornamental swords from the wall display.

Still transfixing her with his gaze, he started flourishing the gleaming sword in wide sweeps around her.

"You've certainly got the courage of a royal princess. It's such a shame that you simply don't look the part."

With each word of his stinging in her ears and with the blade swishing ever closer, Beatrice longed to escape but felt completely ensnared.

"You do want to be beautiful like your aunts, don't you? Well, just like them, you need to trust me and let me make you the best that you can be. If you put your trust in me, you could be even greater than them."

By now, the blade was passing so close to Beatrice that she could feel it brushing against her hair. It was at this moment that Peter burst in.

"What on earth is going on here?" Peter roared.

Startled, Aaron's sword arm flinched. The blade glanced against her, cutting a neat line in her sleeve and just piercing through to her upper arm. Beatrice screamed. At this, Peter ran forward, knocking the chess pieces to the floor. He seized the other bejewelled sword, placing himself between Aaron and Beatrice. Though she longed to cling to her father, she knew that she must be brave and not distract him.

Peter lunged towards Aaron, who parried ably, driving Peter backwards towards Beatrice. Backwards and forwards they fought. Peter had practised fencing since he was a young boy and his skills had been honed when he served in the army during the War of Ten New Moons, as a young man. Beatrice, however, had never seen him fight and was amazed to see her loving father locked in battle.

To begin with, Aaron looked stiff and amateurish in comparison with Peter. However, he seemed to adapt swiftly to the situation. He managed to mimic the Prince's finest swordsmanship, driving him backwards towards the fireplace. Furiously angry, Peter attacked again. Aaron stepped back and tripped over the fallen chess king. Slithering backwards across the polished floor, he hissed,

"You must be mad. Surely you know that I wasn't trying to hurt her."

Peter, who had had a few moments to compose himself replied.

"You may not have intended to injure her with the sword but you certainly meant her harm. You wanted to drain the life out of her just as you have with the rest of your victims. Get out and never come back. If you do, my sword will be waiting for you."

Aaron, now reared to his full height, glared darkly at Peter for a few minutes, before spitting out his poisonous words,

"You can force me to leave the castle at the point of a sword but, trust me, you'll regret treating me like this. I never intended to stay forever. My work here is done and my legacy will remain."

14

—————

Telling Mother

As the sun dipped away, leaving an arc of blushing sky, the darkness started to cloak the castle. Peter stood at the battlements, his shoulders flung back, breathing deeply and peacefully for the first time since he had arrived. He was watching the dark figure riding away between the distant hills, until he finally disappeared. However, his moment of triumph was quickly interrupted by the arrival of Helen.

"What are you doing here? This is where I come in the evenings. What were you watching?"she demanded. As Peter's eyes were still gazing into the distance, she clutched at his arm.

"Answer me! Tell me what you have been doing? Tell me Peter, tell me!"

Suddenly, Peter realised that he did not quite know what to say. He also felt uncomfortable because the wild-eyed face staring at him bore so little resemblance to his beloved sister.

"Actually Helen, not only had that tutor of yours done untold damage to you, Clemence and Isabel and, of course, poor little Molly but he was also attacking Beatrice. I've done the only thing that I could do, given the circumstances. I've banished him."

Peter expected the news of Aaron's attack on Beatrice to incense Helen.

"You've done what!" spat out Helen, in between screams of rage. "How dare you! Aaron was our tutor and you had no right to discipline him, let alone banish him. It's your fault for bringing Beatrice along. If you hadn't brought her, none of this would have happened and we'd still have had our tutor."

After another piercing scream, she howled,

"I'm going to tell Mother!"

Visibly shaking, she turned away from Peter and ran at top speed down the steep spiral stone stairs. Following more carefully in her wake, Peter made his way down to his mother's chamber, hoping to get there before his sister had told her tale. As he approached, however, he could hear the increasingly shrill tones of Helen.

As Peter entered the chamber, Helen screeched,

"Here's your idiot son. You deal with him."

With that, she barged past him and they could hear her feet thudding relentlessly up the stairs.

" Umm...I believe that Helen mentioned that you have taken some action in response to our concern with Aaron," Queen Matilda began, raising one eyebrow as she looked at her son. Peter found himself glancing down at his shuffling feet. He suddenly felt much younger than Beatrice.

"Father asked me to come and sort things out."

"Yes dear. However, I don't think any of us quite envisaged you swashbuckling with him and banishing him from the kingdom. He was actually your sisters' tutor, employed by your father and myself. His behaviour has indeed been causing us grave concern but we wanted you to help us persuade your sisters that they no longer needed him. Really Peter, you haven't changed a bit. I shall never forget that royal visit to Renetia when you were eight and you knocked their young prince to the ground for teasing Helen. It took five years of diplomacy to rectify that outburst and you're still just as impulsive. We wanted you to help us dismiss Aaron, not attack him. Why ever did we name you after your grandfather? You're just as ready to draw a sword as he always was."

"Mother, I can't believe your attitude. Surely you must see what he has done to the girls? Even if you are ignoring that, what about Molly? Don't tell me that a man like that deserves to be treated with any respect or honour. Besides, when I found him, he was brandishing a sword at Beatrice! I don't know what sort of a father you think I am but I'm not going to stand by and watch my daughter being tormented."

"I assure you Peter, I knew nothing of this matter. How is Beatrice? Thank heavens you got there when you did. I couldn't bear to think of anything happening to her."

At this moment, Beatrice's head peered round the door of the chamber.

"I think Father was very brave, Grandma. That tutor was a horrible man. It's only now that he's been sent away that I'm feeling safe again. He has gone, hasn't he, Father?"

"Yes, Beatrice, he's gone for good and everything's going to be all right now. I may be mistaken, but I thought I'd told you to go to bed, young lady."

"It's probably fortunate that I didn't Father, as I think that Auntie Helen's conversation would have woken me up anyway!"

Peter and Queen Matilda exchanged glances and laughed.

15

Stormy weather

Beatrice hurried downstairs. Entering the Great Hall, it was comforting to hear the bustle of the servants preparing for the new day, as they always had done. A broom was scouring dust from the floor and she could hear the sweeping out of the cold ashes from the fireplace of a distant room. There were no screaming, angry voices. However, the sound of Isabel's singing was missing too.

At the far end of the room, Beatrice was surprised to see her father deep in conversation with William, the groom from her home. As she approached, William quickly doffed his cap, using it to mop at the sweat on his brow.

"It's good to see you, your Highness."

Beatrice felt a little foolish. She had only been gone one day.

"Father, what's happening? Why has William followed us here?"

"Well, Beatrice, it turns out that the day we left so hurriedly was a difficult one in the Eastern Province. Torrential rain fell, bursting the banks of the Tovil. Much of the land has been flooded, destroying this year's crops. I'm needed to help organise the rescue of those who are stranded by flood water and make provision for the many more who have no food or places to sleep."

"What about Bright and Mabel, are they all right?" gasped Beatrice, biting her lower lip.

"They're fine your Highness. Gorsebank Castle is on such high ground that it's one of the safest places left in the area."

Peter continued,

"That's precisely why I need to go now and open up our home to all those needing refuge."

"I'll come and help you, Father," Beatrice replied bravely. With all her heart she wanted to stay and enjoy her summer at Great Roseindid. However, she was a royal princess and knew she should do her duty.

"That's kind of you, Beatrice" said Peter, ruffling her hair. "However, this will be no job for a young princess. Besides, I need you here to help your aunties. I think your first task will be to help them to forgive their brother! Apparently they're all sulking in their chambers. On reflection, you may well have the harder task,"

Having sent William ahead to reassure the villagers that he would shortly be with them, Peter also mounted his horse. Standing between the King and Queen, Beatrice watched him go, his hooded cape flowing behind him. She was disappointed that none of her aunties had come to say goodbye. She had hoped that, with Aaron's departure, everything would have returned to normal. Instead of that, the atmosphere in the castle was tense and still, as if a storm was on its way.

Exhausted by the events of the previous night, both the King and the Queen retired to their Solar for a rest. Above her, Beatrice could hear a door slammed shut and the pounding of Helen's feet on the stairs began its relentless cycle. Craving the castle she had always known, Beatrice found herself heading towards the kitchen. She remembered the fun of entering the castle this way with her father last summer.

Entering it quietly, Beatrice breathed in the warm steamy fragrance of venison stew, simmering gently on the range. It was good to be back. Then she caught sight of Cook with her arm round the hunched over figure of Amy, whose usually neat hair was scraped back carelessly into a ponytail. Both were wearing black dresses under their white aprons. Beatrice suddenly remembered Molly. For an instant, she hoped that she could slip away unnoticed. However, Cook's voice made her stand still,

"Beatrice, dear, it's so good to see you. Or should we call you Princess Beatrice now? You've grown into such a fine young lady this year."

Beatrice started to smile but then, for a moment, Aaron's harsh judgement of her as not looking the part of a princess soured her mind. Many times people had complimented her on her looks but this one negative comment stuck in her memory like a thorn. Then, looking back at Cook and Amy, she noticed the tears welling in their eyes. Knowing no words that could heal their wounds, Beatrice rushed forward and threw her arms around Amy.

16

Ambushed

Peter breathed a sigh of relief as he left Great Roseindid Castle behind him. In the event, it was good that he had acted decisively and banished that wretched man at once. Now he was free to sort out the flooding. He had dealt with these crises before; the Eastern Province was notorious for its flooding. That was partly why King Geoffrey had appointed him to the post of Governor. Certainly, it sounded as if the situation was worse than usual this year, but he was confident that he could deal with this problem as effectively as he had done with every other.

Peter was cantering through Brackenhurst Forest when he came to some fallen branches across the bridle path. Slowing his horse to walking pace, so as to make his way around the obstruction, Peter was startled when a figure stepped into his path. He was even more shocked when the stranger darted forward and snatched the reins from him. Immediately, Peter reached for his whip. However, just as swiftly came the words,

"Now, now, your Highness, you always did have a quick temper, even in our army days!"

Although the voice was a little slurred, it was nonetheless familiar. Peter dismounted from the horse and looked closely at the reddened face before him. The long, untamed hair and bushy beard masked his features but the laughing green eyes were unmistakable.

"Harry, I'd forgotten you're working here as the forester. You certainly startled me. How are you, my old friend?"

"It's a good enough way of earning a living and I truly appreciate King Geoffrey giving me this position. Life's still a bit of a struggle, as you can see, but having something to get up for each day certainly helps. You must know what it's like."

For a moment, both men were silent, lost in their private grief. Then Peter shook himself slightly.

"How's your father bearing up? I haven't seen him for years."

"To be honest, I haven't seen him myself since the funerals and I have no wish to. I'm sure his hunting keeps him active and fully occupied. In any case, it's not my family that I wanted to talk to you about, it's yours. It's Princess Helen."

"Helen? What concern is she of yours?" Peter replied stiffly. Harry let out a chuckle, wavering slightly from side to side.

"Keep your sword in its sheath, your Highness. I know how hot-tempered you are, especially when it comes to protecting your sisters. Actually, that's exactly why I'm telling you this. Your sister has taken to wandering, well, marching really, through these woods, as if they were the royal rose gardens. A forest can be a dangerous place for a man, let alone a young woman on her own. Just the other night a man cloaked in black came riding through here shouting and swearing at his horse as though the devil was at his heels."

Peter shuddered involuntarily at this reference to Aaron.

"Harry, if you ever see that man again in this kingdom, do everything you can to drive him out. Most especially keep him away from my sisters. His influence has already killed our maid and he's even attacked Princess Beatrice with a sword. Princess Helen's strange behaviour, not to mention that of her younger sisters, is the fruit of his loathsome tuition. I trust that, in his absence, they will have a swift recovery. You should see no more of Princess Helen in the forest. However, if you do see her, please ensure that she stays safe. I now understand why you ambushed me with those fallen branches. I'm glad you did."

As he had been listening to Peter's account, Harry had unfolded his arms. His fists were clenched and his eyes had lost their merriment.

"Your Highness, by my honour, I will protect your sisters and daughter with my life. Trust me that nothing passing this way shall bring them harm and, if I ever see the dark rider again, he will feel the edge of my sword. There will be no more terrifying of innocent maidens for him. I didn't set any ambush. I was just glad to have the opportunity to speak to you as you passed this way. The storm must have felled the branches."

As the two men parted, silence returned to the glade. A shadowy figure, who had been hiding in the bushes, stepped out and shook the leaves from his black cloak. He murmured to himself,

"I've been called many things in my time but never a storm."

17

The aftermath

Even in the kitchen, the unrelenting thudding of Helen's pattened feet on the stone stairs provided an uneasy pulse.

"I don't understand why Auntie Helen is still rushing around. I thought that the tutor was forcing her to do it but now he's gone."

Sighing deeply, Amy cradled Beatrice's hands in hers very gently. Beatrice could feel that she was shaking slightly.

"Don't be surprised if things don't go back to normal, at least for the time being. That beast of a man has been pouring his poison into their ears for months now. You can't be that ill and just get better overnight. I should know."

Seeing how frail and shaken Amy looked, Cook took over the task of explaining what had happened,

"When Molly became desperately ill, due to that wretched man, Amy took her away from the castle to stay with her sister, hoping that she would make a recovery. However, Molly's mind was too clouded and her body too frail and weak by then to bring her round."

At this they all fell silent. After a while, Beatrice suddenly looked panic-stricken and blurted out,

"You don't think my aunties are going to die, do you?"

Cook and Amy glanced at one another. Amy spoke slowly, as if she was choosing each word with care.

"The Princesses have got every chance of recovery. Your dear father has got rid of the culprit, so now they just need time and help to heal the damage that has been done to their bodies and minds. Even though they have refused to see the physician, we'll be there to help them in any way we can. But Beatrice, you are going to need lots of patience and will have to be very brave. Judging by their mood this morning, they are not going to appreciate our help for a while, however much they need it."

Over the next two weeks, Beatrice often thought back to this conversation and realised how accurate Amy's words had been.

Deprived of dancing with Aaron, Helen had taken to running up and down the castle stairs. The only respite she had from this was when she allowed herself to take long walks away from the castle, deep into the forest.

After screaming at her parents for hours on end, Isabel found that she had entirely lost her voice. Still furiously angry, she vented her feelings through pointing out her commands to her weary parents and servants, poking them if they did not respond immediately to her wishes.

Clemence simply wept. Unable to bear the loss of Aaron, she lost all confidence in herself. Instead of demanding banquets, she spent her days hiding herself away in the dungeon. Only in the middle of the night would she come out and raid the kitchen, carrying away as much food as she could manage. Cook was in despair. She tried preparing a few of Clemence's favourite foods and leaving these out. This was never enough. She tried hiding the bulk of the food but this was always found and taken. She even tried having nothing in her stores, waiting until the next day to replenish them. That night such howling screams could be heard from the kitchen that Cook got up before dawn, gathered provisions from the castle grounds and wearily baked some of Clemence's favourite apple pies and churned cream with milk from the village. By the time that she had finished, she was so exhausted and distressed that she vowed never to leave the castle kitchen empty again.

Beatrice could not bear to think of her beloved Auntie Clemence spending her days alone in the dark dungeon. She would often sit with her. She soon learnt that Clemence would not reply to any of her questions. Even so, Beatrice decided to talk to her. After all, Mabel never answered her in words but she still chatted away to her all the time. She told Clemence all that she had been longing to tell her about Bright and Mabel and the funny things they did and how much she missed them. Clemence gave no sign of listening but sat with her head in her hands, rocking slightly to and fro.

18

Dressing the wounds

Under the canopy of oak trees, the rain fell unevenly. It pooled into leaves until they became so water-laden that they bowed forward, hurtling their gathered droplets to the ground.

Harry was sheltering in his lodge, watching the storm clouds and hoping for a break in the rain. Trapped in these four walls with his thoughts, Harry poured himself another glass of ale. He was sure that there would be no sign of Princess Helen today. He reflected on how inaccurate Peter's predictions had been. If anything, the Princess's marches through the forest had become more regular and more rigorous. He hoped that this unusually bad weather would encourage her to take some rest. She certainly needed it. She looked so grim and gaunt.

Harry sat down heavily with his glass in front of the fading fire. He stirred up the embers roughly with the poker and threw on another log. It looked as if he would be in for a few hours at least.

Suddenly Harry heard a shrill scream. He leapt to his feet, wrapping a cloak around himself and tucking a knife into his belt. He feared that some creature had been caught in a poacher's trap. He hated this part of his job.

Out in the rain, he tried to recall where the sound had come from. Then, to his horror, he heard a woman's voice wailing in pain. It only took him a few minutes to find Helen hunched into a ball on the path, cradling her swelling ankle.

"Your Highness, may I help you?" Harry bent forward to help her to her feet.

"Get away from me! What are you doing here? Who on earth are you?"

"I'm sorry to frighten you, your Highness. I've only come to help. I'm the forester here. I was appointed by your father."

"Well then, he was an idiot. You're the reason that I got hurt in the first place. You left that tree root sticking out of the path. If you'd kept the place tidy, I wouldn't have tripped in the first place and then I wouldn't have to be sitting in the mud talking to you!"

Harry tried for a moment but then he could not hold back the laughter brewing inside him any longer.

"How dare you!" Helen screamed. "No one laughs at a royal princess. Besides, I'm in pain and it's all your fault. I shall have you banished."

At this, Harry roared with laughter again.

"If that's to be my fate, I think I'd better take it upon myself to get you safely bandaged up and back in the castle, so you can tell the King what needs to be done." At this, he scooped up Helen, who was angrily trying to kick him with her uninjured leg, and carried her back to his lodge.

Placing her carefully down in the chair by the fire, Harry poured a little of his ale onto a scrap of cloth and offered to clean the wounds on her hands, which Helen had stretched out to protect herself from the fall.

"Don't touch me. I don't want any of your filthy ale. That's what's wrong with you. You're drunk."

"I'm not asking you to drink it. It will help to clean and heal the wounds, that's all."

"Give it to me then. I'll do it for myself."

Snatching the cloth from Harry, Helen hastily dabbed at the cuts and grazes on the palms of her hands. Involuntarily, she let out a whimper of pain. Gently, Harry took the cloth from her and finished cleaning the wounds. Fetching the bucket of rain water from where it had been gathering outside, he asked her to soak her foot in it.

"I'm a princess. My foot is perfectly clean. Soaking it in your filthy bucket will only make it dirty."

"Princess Helen, you have a injured ankle. I'm trying to reduce the pain and swelling with some cold water, before I bandage it up for you. Do you have a better suggestion?"

Helen snorted but could think of nothing useful to say. She kicked out her injured foot in his direction, crossing her arms. He carefully removed her satin slipper and lowered her foot into the bucket. Helen's face grimaced but she said nothing.

Then, tearing off a strip of old sheet, Harry bound her ankle tightly and raised it, so that it rested on a three-legged stool.

"I don't wish to criticise, your Highness, but these shoes are designed for dancing, not for marching through forests."

"How dare you advise me on my wardrobe choices! I was wearing pattens over them until I fell over your stupid root and now I don't know where they've fallen. I hardly have to take advice from a drunken old vagrant. If you had kept your forest tidy in the first place, I would never have tripped."

"Princess Helen, this is a forest, not a pampered lawn. Trees have roots, believe it or not, just as you have eyes to look where you are going. If you wish to walk around with your nose in the air, may I suggest that you confine yourself to the safety of the

royal castle gardens."

Arching her back and stretching herself to her full seated height, Helen glared at Harry. She had never been spoken to so rudely before.

"I demand that you return me safely to the castle at once. I have nothing further to say to you."With that, she bit her upper lip and turned her head to the right.

"That may be easier said than done, your Highness, since I don't have a gilt carriage to hand. What may surprise you even more is that I haven't had a horse to my name since I lived here. The only livestock

I have kept were a pig and a few chickens, but I don't feel that they would have been up to the challenge. As far as I can see, your options are either me carrying you back or escorting you home in a wheelbarrow."

"I am not travelling in a wheelbarrow!" came the sharp retort.

As the Princess made no further comment, Harry opened the door, gathered her frail form in his arms and strode off towards the castle. The rain had stopped but the path was still slippery underfoot.

As they journeyed, Harry identified the bird calls that surrounded them, giving a good imitation of many of them.

"Now that little fellow in the shabby black suit is a starling. He's a tricky customer, always mimicking the other birds, so you're never quite sure where you are with him. You meet some people like that."

Helen kept silent, even when Harry put her down on the steps of the Mausoleum to catch his breath. However, by the end of their passage through the forest, she was secretly a little sad that their journey together was nearly at an end. For some strange reason, having to hand over control for her safety to this stranger had felt much more reassuring than trying to take care of herself. She had found his description of the birds truly interesting. Much more inspiring than anything her old governess Priscilla had ever taught them about nature.

Remembering Priscilla took her back to her childhood. Suddenly she had a strong desire to be left in the kitchen to be taken care of by Amy, as she and Peter always had been as youngsters when they had been a little too adventurous and got themselves covered in mud, cuts and bruises.

"Take me to the servants' entrance," Helen demanded, once they had passed over the drawbridge, wafting her hand in the direction of the kitchen.

"Don't tell me that after all the threats of banishing me, you're actually a pretentious scullery maid?"

With that, Helen elbowed Harry in the chest until she could wiggle free from his arms. Then, without a word of thanks or goodbye, she hopped across the courtyard into the kitchen.

19

Under the weather

Beatrice woke up with what felt like a piece of holly in her throat. Swallowing drinks soothed it; everything else hurt badly. Trying to speak brought tears to her eyes. The ache was unrelenting. When she sent her breakfast back to the kitchen practically untouched, only a few minutes passed before it reappeared, carried in person by Cook, looking flushed.

"Princess Beatrice, I know it's not my place but I really won't have this kind of behaviour from you. You have got to eat."

With a woeful expression, Beatrice pointed at her throat. She looked at the plate and shook her head sadly. Cook unfolded her arms and gave her a hug.

"If that's all that's wrong, we'll soon have you better. I'll take this away and make you a nice bowl of porridge with plenty of honey. I know what the problem is. You've spent far too long in that damp, dark dungeon, chattering away, trying to help Princess Clemence. It's her decision to be there. You mustn't make yourself ill over it."

Beatrice tried hard not to cry but by now tears were trickling down her hot cheeks.

"You're to go back to bed this minute, Beatrice."

Obediently, Beatrice tucked herself back into the cool, cotton sanctuary of her bed. She felt troubled by the thought of Clemence all alone in the dungeon, thinking that even she had abandoned her.

Suddenly, Beatrice had an idea. Reaching out to her bedside chest, she pulled out a sheet of the parchment she used for letters to her father. It was embossed with pressed flowers. Swiftly she wrote:

"My dearest Auntie Clemence,
I'm so very sorry but I won't be able to visit you today, as I've lost my voice and Cook has sent me to bed. I'm going to miss you so much. Hopefully, I'll feel better soon but I'm not sure how long it will take. I feel really horrible at the moment. I wish things were like they used to be and you could come and sit on my bed and give me a hug. Maybe even tell me a story. I know you're feeling very ill too and that you would if you could.
Your most loving niece, Beatrice"

When Cook returned with a brimming bowl of porridge, Beatrice proudly handed her a letter for Princess Clemence. For a moment, Cook looked a bit puzzled. Then she asked,

"Do you want me to deliver this to the dungeon by any chance?"

Beatrice nodded vigorously. After this she made the effort to sit up and eat her porridge. By then she felt so hot and dazed, that all she could do was sink back into the nest of pillows and sheets and fall into a deep sleep.

When Cook returned to the kitchen, she was startled to see a bedraggled Helen seated on her stool, near the fire. Amy was kneeling at her feet, examining Helen's ankle.

"To be honest, your Highness, it would be foolish of me to unbandage it. Whoever the "idiot" was, he was clearly good at dressing wounds."

"But my ankle was washed in a filthy old bucket by a filthy old forester, who then wrapped it in a bit of torn off old sheet. Surely you're not suggesting that I keep it like this? I wanted you to help me."

"Whatever has happened to you, Princess Helen?" Cook exclaimed. Amy quickly retorted,

"She was out walking around on her own in that forest again. She tripped on a tree root, hurt her ankle and cut her hands. Thankfully some old forester was there and he patched her up and carried her home. I gather that the Princess did not appreciate his bedside manner."

"He was the rudest, most disagreeable person I've ever had to speak to. I told him I'd have him banished, and I will if he ever speaks to me like that or laughs at me again. He knew perfectly well that I was a princess. He even knew my name and yet he had the impertinence to suggest that I was a presumptuous scullery maid!"

Cook's face seemed to be trying hard to look outraged rather than amused. She had pulled up another stool and sat down near Helen. Suddenly she gave a little frown.

"I don't know of any elderly foresters in these parts. You must mean young Harry."

"Oh that's ridiculous. This person had a long shaggy beard and untamed mass of hair. Besides, he stank of ale. Some people are so weak-willed. It's pitiful."

Cook suddenly leapt to her feet.

"It's easy to judge a person when you don't know half that there is to know about them. That poor man's been through more than you could ever imagine and lost more than his mind can bear. That's why he drinks so much ale and maybe of a stronger brew than the ale we serve here in the castle. Besides, if you'll pardon me for saying so, your Highness is not in a position to criticise other people for dealing with things in the way they do. We've all put up with your dancing everywhere and your running up and down the stairs all day long, and yet you begrudge the poor fellow that rescued you his glass of ale."

"What's happened to him then, that you think excuses his appalling lack of manners?"

"I'm not trying to excuse his manners. If he was rude to you, that was shameful. However, unless you think about why people behave as they do, you'll think that everyone's daft. To be honest, the way you behave doesn't make any sense to the rest of us. As for Harry, that poor fellow served bravely in the army alongside your brother. Back then, he was a brave soldier from a fine family. It was when he finally had the chance to go home for some leave…"

At that moment, there was a tapping at the kitchen door. Helen jumped and signalled for Amy to help her into the Great Hall. She had no intention of being caught in the kitchen. She did not want any more odious strangers accusing her of being a servant.

Whilst Cook opened the door a crack, Amy supported Helen as she hobbled away.

20

The response

Beatrice finally stirred. The afternoon sunlight was pouring in across her pillow, warming her face. There was a delicious smell of parsnip and onion soup wafting in her direction from the tray on the window seat. Managing to prop herself up on her pillows, she was surprised to see a sheet of paper laid at the foot of the bed. She could barely read the tiny writing:

"I'm sorry. I feel so guilty that I cannot be with you. I miss you too."

Beatrice clutched the piece of paper to her chest. She read it over and over. Then she started eating her soup, longing to be able to show Cook how thankful she was that she had brought back the note.

Cook took some time in coming and when she arrived she looked hot and flustered.

"I know it's not my place to criticise the Royal family but I can't believe what I've just seen. Princess Helen is limping up and down-stairs with an injured ankle. She's howling with the pain but she just doesn't seem to be able to stop herself. Besides that worry, I've had Anne from the village at the door. She's brought back the guinea pig we gave her daughter when Isabel stopped looking after them. Apparently the poor little thing has stopped eating and they're worried it will die. That's the last thing we need. Amy and I are besides our-selves with all the extra work and the worry of it. To be honest, we need an extra maid now that Molly's gone but every time I hint at it, Amy sobs her heart out. We just end up working all hours trying to look after everyone. Besides, half the food that I prepare disappears in the middle of the night, if you take my meaning."

Beatrice thought this was a good moment to wave the note from Clemence and smile gratefully. Cook however just looked puzzled.

"What's that Beatrice dear, is that another note that you've written?"Beatrice vigorously shook her head and still held out the note.

Cook peered at the letter.

"I'm sorry Beatrice I can't read this but I do believe that it's Princess Clemence's note paper. However did you get it? You didn't go down to the dungeon did you?"

Beatrice shook her head and mimed sleep.

"Well I never. Maybe that pretty note of yours did more good than we could have imagined."

Beatrice quickly picked up another parchment, which she had written whilst waiting for Cook to arrive. She folded the letter and handed it to her, as she was leaving with the tray.

"I don't know what we're going to do with that guinea pig, poor little mite. I would have asked you to help but you've got to stay in bed and look after yourself for once."

~~~~~~~~~~

Amy stood outside the Solar gathering her thoughts. She tidied her grey hair neatly into a bun and took a deep breath. As she leaned close to the door to knock, she could hear Queen Matilda's tired voice remonstrating with Isabel.

"Please dear, do stop unraveling the embroidery from your sleeves. This will be the third perfectly beautiful gown that you've ruined with your fiddling. I know how frustrated you feel about losing your voice but half-starving yourself and moping around all day isn't making it any better, is it Geoffrey?"
~~~~~~~~~~

King Geoffrey was slumped in a carved oak chair. He murmured his agreement. He wished that Peter had not left so quickly. If only he could see the mess that had been left behind.

At that moment came a brisk knocking on the door. Amy entered, looking purposeful. She had something cradled in her hands.

"Your Majesty, please forgive me for disturbing you all. However, a situation has arisen for which I need your help and advice. This morning Anne from the village came to the kitchen door in a terrible state. It turns out that the young guinea pig we gave her daughter has been none too well. In fact, it has stopped eating and unless we do something fast..."Her voice trailed away.

King Geoffrey spoke in a kindly manner,

"Of course, this is all very unfortunate but these things happen. I don't see that there is much that any of us can do. After all, we have had no success with our daughters. What's the likelihood that we can reason better with a guinea pig?"

"Oh Geoffrey, don't be absurd," interrupted the Queen. "Of course we'll do anything we can to help this poor little creature. After all, less than a year ago that this was Isabel's beloved pet. Isabel, what did you call this one? It's the pretty little white one with the black marking."

Isabel shrugged.

"Oh well, I suppose it doesn't matter if you've forgotten its name. Amy, what can we do to help? Shall we summon the ostler?"

"To be honest, your Majesty, though Gerald does wonderful things with the horses, I don't think he knows one end of a guinea pig from the other. When Princess Isabel asked him to sex the guinea pig pups, he complained that that was an impossible task as they are far too small! What this poor little mite needs is constant love and care. Unfortunately, Cook and I and the rest of the servants are working ourselves to the bone and we're still struggling to keep up."

There was an awkward silence. Queen Matilda had guessed that life in the kitchen must be very hard with Molly gone. However, she had tried suggesting the appointment of a new maid several times and knew that this only caused distress. Out of the side of her eye she could see Isabel fiddling even more rigorously with the embroidery on her dress. She longed to give those hands something else to do.

"Isabel!" Queen Matilda reprimanded.

Amy swiftly added,

"That was what Cook and I were thinking. If Princess Isabel would sit and hold the guinea pig on her lap and coax it to eat and drink, it might yet pull through."

Isabel started vigorously shaking her head. Queen Matilda, however, did not appear to notice this as she turned to face Amy.

"I think that's a splendid idea. Isabel has always been so good with animals."

A stifled moan came from Isabel's direction.

"Begging your pardon, your Majesty, it would be most helpful if Isabel could do her nursing of the guinea pig in the kitchen, at least at first. Then Cook and I can lend a hand if we need to. Besides, it seems to have a heavy cold and I've found the steamy air of the kitchen the best remedy for such problems."

"I'm sure that would be in order in the circumstances. Maybe you could give the creature to Isabel and she will join you in a few minutes."

With that, Amy placed the bedraggled guinea pig on Isabel's lap and left swiftly. Since there was little left of Isabel's lap, the poor guinea pig sank in a sea of silk letting out a woeful squeak. Sighing, Isabel reached out her frail fingers and retrieved it, Holding it against her chest, the guinea pig calmed down as it listened to the slow, faint beating of her heart.

"Geoffrey dear, there are a few matters about which I most urgently need your advice. Excuse us, Isabel, your father and I need to spend some time in the Great Hall. I'm sorry to leave you like this but I'm sure you'll cope very well. I think that Amy will be looking forward to your arrival in the kitchen as soon as you can manage it. I do hope the poor little thing makes a swift recovery."

By the time that Isabel had mustered the energy to look up at her mother, both she and King Geoffrey had left. Having to hold the guinea pig with both hands, Isabel was unable to pick away further at her gown cuff. To her amusement though, it started nibbling at the threads which she had loosened. Isabel tried to smile but the skin around her jutting cheek bones was too taut. In a voice smaller than the guinea's pig's, Isabel whispered,

"Oh Cleo, I do remember you. You were always my favourite. You've got to get better. I don't know how I'm going to manage it but I will take you to the kitchen and look after you."

Dread welled up inside Isabel at the thought of all this effort. Her head flopped forward and she started crying. Cleo gave a sneeze. With a groan, Isabel gathered the poorly guinea pig into one hand and used the other to prise herself out of her chair. She tottered towards the kitchen.

21

At her bedside

As Beatrice was drifting back to sleep, she heard the door of her chamber creaking open very slowly. Her eyes were almost too heavy to open but she heard someone tiptoeing softly towards the bed. Something landed lightly on the quilt above her feet.

With huge effort, Beatrice managed to peep over the edge of the crisp cotton sheet folded back over the quilt. To her disappointment, all she could see of Clemence was her retreating back, wrapped securely in her Christmas shawl. She tried to call after her, but nothing came out. By then she could hear Clemence's footsteps fading away along the Gallery. For a moment she sat up in bed, her eyes stinging with tears at the pain of having tried to talk. Instead of feeling boiling hot, as she had a moment ago, she started to shiver.

Grasping the note, Beatrice retreated back under the covers. The writing was still tiny:

"Cook told me how ill you are with your sore throat and fever. She asked me to help you but I'm not sure if I'll be able to. I'll do what I can. Please get better soon."

When Beatrice awoke, the pale light of dawn was coaxing its way through the ornate, stained glass window, leaving dappled patches of blue, red and gold across the quilt. Suddenly, she noticed someone's head leaning against the right hand side of the bed. Someone with dark, curly hair had fallen asleep on the floor with their back to the bed. Beatrice longed to call out Clemence's name but only a painful croak emerged when she tried. Instead, she tugged lightly at the bedspread, until the figure stirred.

Turning around to face Beatrice, but without getting up, Clemence lolled against the bed. Beatrice was, for a moment, glad that her painful throat excused her from having to say anything, as the sight before her left her speechless. For the first time since she was back at the castle, Beatrice could clearly see Clemence's face. Her dimpled smile was lost in a wilderness of hollow cheeks. Her arms were slightly trembling but Beatrice was unsure whether Clemence was feeling the cold or struggling with difficult feelings.

Beatrice managed a beautiful smile and stretched out her arms towards her auntie. With something of a struggle, Clemence got to her feet and enveloped Beatrice in a frail hug.

"Please try to have some of your breakfast, Beatrice. Cook has left it here with me and asked me to give you whatever help you need."

Wavering slightly under the weight, Clemence put the breakfast tray on Beatrice's lap, propping her up in the bed with pillows so that she was supported. Beatrice sipped her honeyed wine happily and tried hard to eat her bowl of porridge with honey. Even this rasped down her swollen throat. Seeing how painful Beatrice was finding it to swallow, Clemence loosely clasped her hand,

"You're a brave girl, much braver than me. You've done really well and Cook will be proud of you. I'm proud of you."

Beatrice gave a smile but by now her head was beginning to swim again with the effort. Lightly touching her forehead, Clemence exclaimed,

"Oh Beatrice, you're burning up. You must feel awful. "

Gently she rearranged the pillows so that Beatrice could sink back to sleep.

22

A break for freedom

Isabel was hunched in the corner of the pantry with Cleo nestled in her lap. She had found the cooking smells far too overwhelming. Every now and then Cook would bring in a pan of steaming water laced with balsam, to help the guinea pig breathe more easily. Besides, this was much quieter than the bustling kitchen, so she could concentrate fully on her nursing duties and even whisper words of encouragement out of earshot of Cook and Amy.

Isabel kept cleaning the drying catarrh from the guinea pig's nose with a damp cloth. In between, she tempted it to eat little sprigs of parsley and freshly washed lettuce from the kitchen garden. Cook suggested dandelion leaves but, when Sam went to look, the gardener sent him back with the message that no such weeds were permitted in the grounds of Great Roseindid Castle.

Even without the help of dandelions, the little guinea pig seemed much restored in health. Cook was quick to point out that Cleo had helped herself by taking advantage of all the good food that was provided for her. Isabel ignored this comment and kept stroking Cleo's pretty pink ears.

"Mind you, your Highness, she's going to need help for a few days yet to get her back on her feet properly."

Isabel glanced in Cook's direction and tried to smile.

At lunchtime, when Cook left a steaming bowl of parsnip and onion soup near at hand to ease Cleo's breathing, Isabel could resist no longer. To her relief, Cook had conveniently left a spoon in the bowl. Although this was not food rich enough to be fitting for a princess. Isabel ravenously ate it all. By tea time another bowlful was provided. Despite still feeling full, Isabel managed to eat it. She was growing weary of being almost too weak to lift Cleo onto her chest. She also hated sitting on the unforgiving wooden stool in the kitchen, which burnt against her frail frame, despite the layers of petticoat and gown.

Even in the noisy kitchen, Isabel could hear the relentless tapping of Helen's staff echoing down the stone stairs. Helen's constant exercise had already been making everyone tense. Now that she was limping around the castle on an injured ankle and refusing treatment from either the physician or the barber surgeon, tempers were getting frayed. Queen Matilda regularly pleaded with her to stop but to no avail. Amy risked the royal displeasure by trying to stop her. Stepping in front of her that morning, as Helen tried to leave her chamber, Amy had firmly escorted her back to her bed and insisted that she sat down.

"Princess Helen, if you don't take the weight off that ankle it will not heal properly. Who knows, you might never be able to dance on it again."

"I'm perfectly able to make my own decisions. I do need advice from the kitchen."

Nevertheless, Helen had remain seated for a while, allowing Amy to brush her hair over and over and eventually plait it into an intricate style. However, as soon as Amy left to help Cook prepare lunch, Helen had resumed her limping.

<center>~~~~~~~~~~</center>

Breathing deeply with the pain, Helen reached the battlements. From her perch, she could see the figure of Harry leaving the castle. King Geoffrey appeared to be walking a little distance with him, deep in discussion. Helen felt flustered. Surely the only reason that that man would have visited the castle would have been to apologise or to enquire after her health. If so, why had nobody bothered to inform her. Naturally, she would have refused to see him. However, she would like to have had the opportunity to give that message herself.

As fast as she could manage, Helen hobbled down the stairs, intent on confronting the King and Queen. However, by the time she reached the door of the Solar, she was breathless and feeling faint. She steadied herself for a moment against the oak door. To her surprise, it pushed open a little, so that she could hear them speaking.

"I can't believe the nerve of that man, after all that Peter said to him. How could he presume to hunt in our forest? Does he know no shame?"

"I suppose that Peter banished him from the castle, not the kingdom. Still you'd think he would have the commonsense to stay well away from here."

"Thank goodness Harry had the good sense to warn us. Whatever happens, Helen is not to be allowed out of the grounds at present. Nor are any of the girls to be told that that despicable man is so close by!"

Helen started breathing more quickly. She had no intention of being penned up in the castle. Besides, Peter had had no right to banish Aaron. More than anything else, she longed to see him again. He would understand how unhappy everyone was making her with their petty restrictions on her exercise.

Tightly clutching the wooden railing, Helen made her way grimly down the staircase to the entrance, wincing each time her swollen ankle touched the ground. Despite the pain, she managed to cross the drawbridge and set out towards the forest.

23

The deadly dagger

Dusk cloaked Helen's disappearance. She had never ventured into the forest this late before. Shadows danced around her, making it hard for her to find the path she usually took. An owl startled her. She hoped that Harry was snugly settled in front of his fire. She paused in her tracks. For a fleeting moment, the image of Harry seemed sharper than her memory of Aaron. Then she shook herself. How absurd to be thinking of some filthy old forester when she was on her way to see her beloved tutor again.

Suddenly there was a rustling in the bushes. To her relief, a familiar figure stepped onto the path. Aaron's fine frame was silhouetted against the darkening sky between two ivy-entwined trees. At that moment, she recognised this as the place where she had tripped previously. Despite feeling embarrassed at her lameness, she started hobbling towards him. He was standing in a statuesque pose. Only his granite grey eyes moved, surveying her from head to toe. As she got to within a few feet of him, Helen saw Aaron more clearly. She was startled. His forehead and hands were furrowed, his cheeks hollow. The grey of evening seemed to have crept into his raven black hair. There was no warmth of recognition in his gaze. However, his unblinking eyes held hers captive.

"Is that really you, Helen? You disappoint me. Why on earth are you hobbling along with a stick like some old woman?"

"Oh Aaron, it's been terrible since you left. I couldn't endure dancing alone again, so instead I climbed the stairs and walked through this forest. That is, until I tripped over a tree root and injured my ankle. Everyone's been ordering me to stop walking but I haven't, really I haven't. I've kept exercising though it's been agonisingly painful. I knew you'd want me to."

"Call that exercise? Crippling along with a stick. After all that I worked so hard to achieve with you. You disgust me. You're just lazy. Why haven't you been dancing?"

Helen, by now, was clenching her hands so tightly that her fingernails dug into the palms of her hands. She was distraught that Aaron felt that she had betrayed him so very badly.

"I'll dance if you want me to."

Snatching the stick from Helen, Aaron flung it into the bushes angrily. Then he gripped her tightly by the hand and started whirling her around the glade.

Unable to keep up with the momentum, Helen's injured ankle was dragged over and wrenched sideways across the uneven ground. She heard herself screaming out uncontrollably with the searing pain. Then the night seemed swiftly to engulf her sight, to the accompaniment of a deafening drone in her ears. As she collapsed, Aaron let go of the dead weight in his arms, allowing her to crash to the ground.

Hearing the piercing screams, Harry put down his jug of ale. His army sword had been retrieved from the rusty metal trunk by his bed and polished and sharpened. His fingers fumbled with the buckle on the sword belt. Swaying slightly, he made his way into the gloom.

Harry knew exactly which way to go this time. The scream was all too familiar. For a moment, he wondered if Helen had tripped over the same root. He chuckled to himself, imagining how far she would threaten to banish him this time. Then he remembered the reason for the sword. Soberly, he hastened his pace through the thicket.

As Harry approached the clearing, he saw the limp figure of Helen being dropped by the dark stranger. The latter heard his approach and glared up at him with fiercely defiant eyes, like those of a cornered fox.

Suddenly, Aaron pounced, drawing a dagger from his belt. Harry stepped back, parrying his advance with his swiftly drawn sword. Again Aaron attacked.

As Harry backed protectively towards the Princess, he tripped over the tree root, falling backwards against her. Without hesitation, Aaron leant over his victim and plunged a dagger into Harry's chest, aimed at the heart. Then he carefully wiped his dagger clean on Harry's jacket and straightened himself up. He turned away, returning the dagger to his belt and uncoiling his tense neck and shoulders from his recent exertion.

"So much for the protector of princesses! Now it's just the precious Prince himself for me to deal with." As he left, the night swallowed him up.

24

The missing princess

Coming round swiftly when Harry fell against her, Helen had witnessed the attack on him as if in a nightmare. Petrified with horror, she had lain still until Aaron disappeared. She was terrified that her thudding heart would betray her to him. She could feel her sleeve becoming saturated. She wished more than anything else that she could have saved Harry. It was unbearable to think that he was dead and that it was her fault.

Helen had never felt so terribly alone before. For the first time in her life, she felt utterly consumed by fear. Despite being completely betrayed by her former tutor, Helen had no time now for anger. It was loss that overwhelmed her to the very soul. After a few minutes of feeling paralysed by her grief, Helen managed to sit up. Harry's body was to the right of her. She could see how drenched his tunic was over the heart.

"Oh, Harry, I'm so, so sorry. It's all my fault. You've done nothing but look after me and I've been nothing but horrible to you. If I hadn't been so stupid, you'd never have had to fight Aaron and you would have spent a cosy evening in your lodge. What have I done. . ?"

As Helen's words turned into sobs, she rested her head against his chest. Suddenly, she felt some movement and a rather slurred voice chuckled,

"I couldn't have put it better myself, your Highness. Mind you, if I had said as much, you no doubt would have had me banished to the moon!"

Startled, Helen sat bolt upright.

"But you're covered in blood. You were stabbed in the heart. How can you possibly be alive?"

"Your Highness, I may at times drink rather more than I should, but even my blood is not pure ale. It was my leather wineskin that your tutor pierced, not my heart."

"If that was all that happened, why on earth are you still lying there, frightening me half to death? Some protector you are!"

"To be honest, although the dagger missed my heart, it skewed upwards and dug in under my shoulder. I have lost some blood along with the ale. Alcohol can't solve all my problems, it seems."

In the darkening forest, Helen knelt beside Harry. She had no idea what to do next.

~~~~~~~~~~~

Cook was so relieved to see that the second bowl of soup had been eaten by Isabel that she could have cried with joy. When it came to supper time, she handed a large bowl brimming with soup to Isabel and a plate of freshly baked bread.

"You're doing so well today, Princess Isabel. You'll soon be well again at this rate."

Turning to go, Cook flinched as she heard the clatter of pewter dishes being flung to the floor.

Clutching the frightened guinea pig tightly to her shoulder, Isabel stormed out of the kitchen. Strengthened by a day of eating, she was able to march swiftly up the stairs to the Solar. Without knocking, she burst in. She strode to where King Geoffrey was reclining by the fire and thrust the guinea pig, squeaking loudly, onto his lap.

"Maybe you'd like to spend a week living like a servant, your Majesty. Then they could force-feed you like a peasant with stupid bowls of soup all day long!"
~~~~~~~~~~~

"Isabel, how dare you speak to your father like that! What's more, you were meant to be nursing this poor little creature back to health and yet here you are frightening it half to death."

Enraged, Isabel started screaming. A raw, throat-wrenching howl followed her retreating figure along the Gallery to her chamber.

"Geoffrey dear, I do believe that Isabel's voice may have returned! Perhaps Beatrice would look after the guinea pig until Isabel's temper cools."

"That seems sensible my dear. At least all seems quiet again for the time being."

For a few moments, both King and Queen relaxed.

"Geoffrey, there's something wrong. Something's missing."

"Helen!" they both exclaimed. The stone stairs were chillingly quiet.

"Perhaps Amy has prevailed on her to take some rest again."

Even Queen Matilda did not sound as if she was convinced by her own suggestion. Nevertheless, she hastened to Helen's chamber, hoping to find her daughter safe and well. She soon returned.

"Geoffrey, there's no sign of her! I've summoned the servants to search the castle and grounds. You don't think that man has been here again do you?"

"Sit down my dear," King Geoffrey replied, guiding his trembling wife towards a chair. "I'm sure that there will be a perfectly reasonable explanation for this. Here we are spending our days wishing that Helen would stop trailing up and down those wretched stairs. When she finally shows the sense to stop, we start to panic. We're just a pair of old fools, my dear."

"You speak for yourself! It's your fault for letting our home be so pitifully protected. It's more like living in a cottage than a castle. The moat is dry and you've even let the arrow slits become choked with ivy. Now you're just sitting there petting a guinea pig while our daughter may be in mortal danger." By now, Queen Matilda's voice had reached a piercing pitch. "Besides, where are Clemence and Isabel, not to mention little Beatrice?"

Fortunately, Amy arrived and was able to reassure the Queen that Clemence was caring for Beatrice, who was still ill in bed. As for Isabel, she had been crying in her chamber but was now calming down and asking for Cleo.

"However, your Majesty, we've searched the castle and gardens thoroughly and there is no sign of Princess Helen. I've sent Sam to alert Harry, just in case she has taken an evening walk further afield. They're both good fellows and I'm sure they'll soon find her."

~~~~~~~~~~

Sam's hands were shaking so much that he had found it hard to saddle the horse. Fear and anger were battling in his mind. Thoughts of Molly, which he would normally have tried to stifle, were erupting within him. Aaron was out there somewhere in the dark and Princess Helen was lost. He had not been able to save Molly. Now there was a chance to save the Princess but he felt small and horribly afraid. Letting everyone down was unthinkable yet, with the strange drunken forester as his only ally, he feared that he would fail.

In the end, Sam decided that no amount of thinking and worrying was going to help him save the Princess. He might not be a tall, strong man or a brave soldier, but he would do his best and that would have to be enough.

As Sam reached the edge of the forest, he was engulfed in darkness. The stars were hidden by overlying branches and the moonlight only left stale milky puddles of light. He had never come into the forest at night. He had been born in Rosenwell village and had enjoyed playing in the safety of the golden fields. Only Fred and Tom, the most reckless of the village boys, had ever ventured into the night-drenched forest. They came back with tales of wizards and goblins behind almost every tree. However, they had never wanted to go back.

Holding the reins wound tightly around his right hand, Sam edged forward. He wondered how he was meant to find Harry's lodge in the
~~~~~~~~~~

darkness, let alone the missing Princess. A nearby owl seemed only too ready to mock Sam for his lack of progress. Shocked by the sound, he had pulled the horse to a standstill. Now that there was no longer the sound of hooves in the undergrowth, he could hear a faint sobbing.

"Princess Helen, is that you?" he whispered. There was no answer but he could still hear the sobbing. Dismounting from his horse, he carefully picked his way towards the sound.

As the trees gave way to a small clearing, the moonlight was able to pour through, revealing Princess Helen hunched over a man's outstretched figure.

"Princess Helen, it's Sam. I've come to take you home."

Turning swiftly towards him, Helen cried out,

"Oh Sam, I'm so glad to see you. I need your help. Harry's been badly hurt and I don't know what to do."

Forgetting his fears of Aaron and the dark forest, Sam began to breathe more easily. Princess Helen was alive and needed his help. He took off his cloak and wound it tightly around Harry's chest, before hoisting him onto his horse. He then helped Helen to mount behind Harry and asked her to support him, as Harry was lolling to one side. Holding the reins, Sam walked alongside the horse, leading them all back to the safety of the castle.

25

A mysterious stranger

As Beatrice finally drifted into a deep sleep, Clemence left, closing the door softly behind her. As usual, she had waited all day without eating, craving her nightly feast in the dark kitchen. She was horrified to see that candles were lit and to hear voices coming from the open door. She wanted to stay well away from everyone but hunger drove her on. Stepping into the warmth of the kitchen, she drank in the scent of onion broth.

To her amazement, the stable boy was sitting at the kitchen table opposite Cook. He was dipping a large crust of bread into a plate of the broth. He seemed to be giving an account of something so exciting that he did not pause for a second in his storytelling, even when he was munching.

"It was just good that I came along when I did. Princess Helen was half-dead and that poor old forester looked like he was done for. Goodness knows what would have happened next, what with that beast roaming the forest. When I got there..."

"Princess Clemence! I didn't see you there. Don't pay any heed to young Sam. He's had a bit of a fright, that's all."

Clemence looked blankly at Cook and then went to the pantry, which was always stocked with pies and pastries. There was nothing there. In a sudden rage, she returned to the main kitchen.

"What's the meaning of this? Why is there no food left?"

Cook was taken aback by the wild, staring eyes defying her.

"Oh your Highness, I'm sorry. It's been such a night, I've had no time for baking. Even the bits I had left were needed to feed those coming back to the castle. There's plenty of broth, if you'd like a bowl."

"That's not what I want. How dare you!" screamed Clemence, nearly knocking the soup from its perch over the fire as she pushed her way past Sam. Tripping over a stool, she fell onto the flagged floor. Shoving Cook away, as she tried to help her to her feet, Clemence stumbled off alone towards the dungeons, sobbing uncontrollably. Steadying herself against the stonewall for a moment, she snatched at something from a gloomy alcove and slipped it in her pocket.

~~~~~~~~~~

After a sleepless night, Clemence slowly made her way up to Beatrice's room. Cook met her at the door.

"Princess Clemence, I'm so sorry about last night. I was at my wits' end with all the comings and goings. I hope you don't mind but I've made an extra bowl of porridge for you, if you would like to join in with Beatrice. I'm sorry that it is not food fit for a princess but, as young Beatrice has found, it slips down the throat nicely with a bit of honey."

At first Clemence felt cold with fear but she managed not to hand the bowl back. When Cook had left, she looked over at Beatrice, propped up in bed, trying hard to swallow the steaming porridge.

Without saying anything, Clemence slid the spare bowl closer to her and took a tiny spoonful from the edge of the dish. It tasted wonderful, sweeter than any honeyed dessert she had tasted before. Unable to restrain herself any longer, Clemence swiftly finished the plateful and pushed the empty dish far from her, so that she did not have to look into the empty cavern that was left in the bowl. She began to feel guilty and uncomfortable.

However, when Clemence glanced over at Beatrice, she was amazed at the joy and pride in her niece's face. Suddenly Clemence felt
~~~~~~~~~~

fuller than she had after any of her midnight feasts. However, this was a fullness of joy rather than of guilt at what she had let herself do.

~~~~~~~~~~~

Amy was exhausted. She had sat up all night looking after Harry. The one consolation had been his healthy and seemingly bottomless appetite. He had lost a lot of blood before the barber-surgeon had arrived to bandage him up properly. However, she shuddered to think what would have happened but for the leather wineskin under his jerkin.

Amy understood why Princess Helen had mistaken him for an old man. His ash-blond hair and long beard were tangled, like a lion's mane. His skin was weather-beaten and his clothes ragged and shabby. It was only when he finally looked directly at Amy with his bright green eyes, that she could see the fine young man beneath the weathered shell.

"Don't worry my dear, you'll soon be feeling better. The worst of your injuries is a small broken bone to the side of your shoulder and you'll just have to be patient and wear your arm in a sling for a week or so. King Geoffrey says that you should stay here, so that you can be cared for until you are properly better. Besides, you're an honoured guest after what you did for the Princess. The King also insists that you have some of Prince Peter's clothes to wear while you are staying with us. Yours have been drenched in blood and ripped apart, so that we could get to your injuries. I'm afraid you'll have to put up with me helping you get cleaned up and dressed though."

Several hours later, a figure emerged from the chamber. Red-faced with embarrassment as well as sunburn, Harry descended the stairs, his right arm tightly bound in a high sling. He had been told by Amy that he was allowed to go anywhere on the ground floor.

To his disappointment, there was no one in the Great Hall. Feeling too ill at ease to make himself at home in one of the stately chairs carved with lion-headed arm-ends and pawed feet, he decided to make his way to the kitchen.
~~~~~~~~~~~

The main kitchen was empty. However, Harry spotted familiar auburn hair, swept into an unexpectedly elaborate, plaited style, with ringlets at each side of the head. The Princess was seated in the pantry with her back to him. She was hunched over something on her lap and seemed to be talking to it. As he approached, he was amazed to see a plump little creature being fed a carrot almost as large as it was.

"I'd guessed you were a pretentious scullery maid but I never imagined that you spent your days overfeeding a pet rat!"

Isabel, clutching the guinea pig to her shoulder, leapt to her feet and spun round to meet her accuser. She was startled to see a handsome, well-dressed young man leaning over her.

"I'm so sorry miss. You'll think I'm mad but I mistook you for a princess."

"Is that really how you address a princess? I've certainly never been spoken to like that before."

"I may be mistaken but I have a feeling that I'm addressing Princess Isabel. My sincere apologies. For a moment I thought I was speaking to Princess Helen."

"How do you come to know my sister?"

"I've had the honour of meeting her on several occasions in the forest. Please excuse me, your Highness, and forgive me for insulting both you and your pet - whatever it is. It looks even more offended that you do."

Left alone with the wheeping guinea pig, Isabel decided that it was time that she visited her elder sister. Knocking briskly on Helen's chamber door, Isabel waited for a response. As there was none, she marched in. Her sister was curled up asleep in bed. After the terrible ordeal of the previous night, Amy had left her to get as much sleep as possible.

Helen awoke feeling slightly sick and dazed. The pain in her ankle seared through her, as an unpleasant reminder of the agony of the previous night. She was puzzled to see Isabel perched on the edge of her bed, looking at her accusingly.

"What have you been up to in the forest?"

"I'm so sorry I went to see him. It was foolish of me. I didn't want anyone to get hurt on my account. I never want to see him again."

"Well that's all very well to say, what with him wandering willy-nilly around the castle, insulting me and Cleo."

"Aaron's here!" Helen gasped, pulling the bedclothes tightly around her neck.

"Not Aaron, the nobleman that you been consorting with."

"What are you going on about? I heard that Aaron was in the forest so I crept out last night to try to see him."

"You went to see Aaron without me? How dare you!"Helen sensed that Isabel was working herself up to a scream. She quickly interrupted.

"Yes, I did, and I wish with all my heart that I hadn't. That man's evil. Peter was right all along. He dragged me around like a ragdoll and threw me away when he tired of me. Then he tried to kill the poor old forester."

"How many men do you meet in the forest? No wonder Clemence and I aren't allowed to go there. It's not fair!" Isabel wailed.

"Forget about the forest for a moment, who's this nobleman that's been wandering around the castle?"

"You should know. Surely there aren't so many men that you meet in the forest that you can't work out who it is."

With that, Isabel swept Cleo off the quilt, which she had been gently nibbling, and left with a loud slam of the door. Her footsteps trailed off in the direction of her mother's chamber.

26

The intruder

Clemence could see that Beatrice's fever had broken. Her niece was now able to sit propped up in bed for longer periods. She could whisper without hurting her throat too much. However, she was starting to get bored.

By mid-morning, Beatrice had asked her to retrieve the smaller chest of board games from the Council Chamber. Clemence had shuddered a little when Beatrice chose Fox & Geese. There had been many long evenings when Aaron had proved his supremacy over Clemence by outfoxing her poor defenceless gaggle of geese. One by one, her geese got spread around the board, allowing him to destroy them with merciless ease. However, she knew that Beatrice had many fond memories of playing this game with her, so she fought back her painful thoughts and spread out the game on the bedspread.

By the time that Cook arrived with lunch, both Clemence and Beatrice were in fits of giggles. For the third time, Clemence had let her fox be hen-pecked, or rather goose-pecked, into a corner by Beatrice's determined army of geese, who having cut off his retreat in all directions, claimed the victory.

Clemence had been so absorbed in the game that, for the first time in months, she had entirely forgotten about food. When two steaming plates of huntsman's pie arrived on a tray, it seemed only natural to have the meal with Beatrice, though she quickly pushed her plate under Beatrice's when she had finished.

~~~~~~~~~~~~

Isabel was sitting bolt upright in the chair opposite the Queen, with her arms folded. The only thing that was moving was her right knee which was visibly juddering up and down under her gown.

"For the sixth time Isabel, I do not know of any suitor for Helen, nor do we have any noblemen staying at the castle. The only guest that I am aware of is that poor, broken-down old forester who your father invited to stay."

"But I saw him, I tell you! He was in the kitchen calling Cleo a rat and me a scullery maid."

With a deep sigh and her left hand pressed to her forehead, Queen Matilda slowly replied,

"Isabel, when you were a little girl we admired your imaginative stories. You are now a woman of thirteen and you really need to start acting like it. I know that you are jealous of your sister but telling me these ridiculous tales about her is doing you no favours. I don't want to hear another word."

As the Queen turned to go, Isabel let out one of her piercing screams.

Both were amazed when this was swiftly followed by the sound of boots thundering up the stairs and a hammering on the chamber door.

"Helen, is that you? Are you all right?"

When there was no immediate answer, the door was flung open and Harry burst in, knocking into the Queen.

"Who exactly are you, young man, and why are you dressed in my son's clothes?"

"Please forgive me, your Majesty. The last time I heard a scream like that, it was Princess Helen in mortal danger in the forest. I should not have come upstairs and I certainly should not have intruded in such a manner. As far as Peter's clothes are concerned, your house-keeper had assured me that the King wished me to borrow them dur-
~~~~~~~~~~~~

ing my stay, since my own clothes had been ruined in the conflict. I didn't mean to cause offence."

"Are you really on first name terms with the Prince?"

"I do beg your pardon, your Majesty, for yet another mistake. Having served alongside your son in the war, I tend to think of him as a friend. However, in future I shall always address him as Prince Peter. Please excuse me before I fall headlong into another blunder."

"Or senior member of the Royal family," the Queen muttered. However, she swiftly regained her poise.

"I am delighted to meet you and thank you from the bottom of my heart for rescuing Princess Helen on two occasions. We should be honoured if you would care to join us for dinner this evening and on the other days of your stay with us."

Realising that his presence was no longer required, Harry gave a smart bow and retired as quickly as he could.

Left on their own, Isabel rearranged the folds of her skirt, biding her time for the apology to come. When her mother said nothing, Isabel said with cutting clarity,

"Oh well, it's nice of Helen to take it upon herself to be so gracious towards the old and infirm of the kingdom. That poor old forester seems to follow her around like a pet hound."

"I am somewhat surprised by what a sprightly young fellow he is. What a shame it is that nowadays it is only Father and myself who can be bothered to dine in the Great Hall. It will be such a disappointment for him. Nevertheless, I'm sure Father and I can entertain him with conversation about the weather and which crops should be grown."

Seeing Isabel rolling her eyes at the prospect, Queen Matilda continued,

"Of course, as the evening wears on, my favourite topic with guests has always been the charming escapades of three naughty little Princesses. The tale of you falling in the..."

"I don't wish to hear any more and I'm sure he wouldn't either. I may come along myself, just to be charitable."

27

A knock at the door

For Helen, who had dozed off again after the visit from Isabel, it seemed as if no time had passed until her mother rapped smartly on the door and entered without waiting for a reply.

"This chamber is getting like Rosemorton on market day! What do you want, Mother?"

'I'm glad that your wit has recovered as well as the rest of you, after last night's escapade. Please don't ever go into the forest on your own again. No matter how charming the forester may be, he can't always be expected to be on hand to rescue you from your latest scrape."

"Oh Mother, please don't listen to Isabel's tale about some handsome stranger and then assume that this imaginary figure is a description of that old goat of a forester that rescued me."

"Well, my dear, if that crude description is how you rate the person who saved your life, I despair of you ever finding any suitor suitable."

"Oh Mother, I know you're getting rather more mature but surely you don't expect me to admire the looks of someone who'd make Father look like a sprightly youth?"

"That's quite enough of this ridiculous conversation, Helen. Isabel has graciously agreed to attend dinner tonight in the Great Hall in honour of your rescuer. I expect no less of you. Please dress formally for dinner, unless you want to be completely outshone by Isabel. Quite frankly, she seems to be quite an admirer of your poor old goat."

With that, Queen Matilda left and Helen chuckled to herself,

98

"If Isabel is going to be ingratiating herself upon that old forester, this will indeed be a sight worth going to dinner for."

Clemence, however, declined Queen Matilda's invitation to dinner. She was just beginning to cope with eating her meals with Beatrice. She had no intention of risking her progress by attending a banquet, especially with a stranger present. She feared that she would either eat nothing or that she would eat far more than the rest of the guests put together. Besides, though Beatrice's health was becoming much better, she was still too weak for a formal banquet, much to Clemence's relief.

As they continued their games of Fox and Geese, Clemence noticed how Aaron's tactics had mirrored the way that he had behaved with the Royal family. Subtly dividing them from one another, each had become vulnerable to his attack.

Clemence suddenly remembered Sam's comment about Helen being attacked by a beast in the forest. She felt a wave of shame that she had been so consumed by her own hunger at the time that she had not even stopped to ask what had happened and if her sister had been harmed. Excusing herself, she slowly made her way along the Gallery to Helen's room. Tapping lightly against the door, she was taken aback by the shouted response,

"If you're trying to marry me off to some senile old forester, I don't want to know!"

Clemence felt a little puzzled but decided to let curiosity get the better of her. She went into her sister's chamber.

"Oh, it's just you Clemence. At least you won't start accusing me or ordering me around like the rest of them do."

Encouraged by this compliment, Clemence sat down on the edge of the bed.

"I just came to ask if you were safe and well. I heard something about a beast attacking you in the forest last night. I'm so sorry."

For a moment, Helen hung her head. Then she started speaking softly,

"It's me who should be apologising to you, Clemence. I heard that Aaron was in the forest and I was so frustrated with everyone telling me what to do, that I felt that I had to escape and see him. I thought he would make things better but he only made them much worse. I wish he had never come to be our tutor. He promised so much to each of us but then he took away the good things we already had. I can hardly shuffle around now, let alone dance, because of the terrible pain in my ankle. Looking back, all I wanted was to dance beautifully, just like Isabel wanted to be the best singer. We all know how he wrecked her lovely voice with his harsh rules and exercises. I've never thought of it before Clemence, but what did he promise you?"

"Confidence to be able to be myself without feeling shy or having to please other people all the time. He gave me a strong voice so that I could demand the things I wanted. The problem was, that for all the confidence I gained with other people, he leeched far more from me with his constant jeering and criticisms. He made me feel that I was so pathetic that I could only survive through him and by using the hateful tactics that he taught me. I felt like an empty cavern with only his cruel voice echoing through me."

"Would you have tried to go and see him in the forest, if you'd been the one to overhear that he was there?"

"Until recently, I would certainly have escaped from the dungeon to meet with him. However, whether Beatrice realises it or not, she has helped me to appreciate that I am far more than an empty cavern, unleashing a monster from within whenever hunger gets the better of me."

Helen sat back, stunned. That was, in some way, similar to how she had come to feel about her exercise, since Aaron had drained all pleasure from it, turning it into an unbearably heavy burden. She had no idea that her gentle sister had been suffering so much.

"Clemence, you need to remember that you are worth every bit of the same kindness that you so readily give to everyone else."

Clemence instinctively shrank away from the compliment. It was time for her to get back to Beatrice and to leave Helen to prepare herself for whatever the evening had to bring.

<h1 style="text-align:center">28</h1>

An evening's entertainment

Queen Matilda enjoyed her view of the banqueting table. The pewter dishes were interwoven with vases of pink peonies, as large and luxurious as the dishes which appeared. King Geoffrey sat at the head of the table, looking more relaxed and cheerful than he had for over a year. It was a shame that Clemence was absent but at least Cook had given assurances that she was beginning to eat more sensibly.

Both Helen and Isabel had dressed exquisitely for dinner. Their faces were still hollow-cheeked and their beautiful auburn hair lacked its usual lustre but at least they were both there, sitting at the table and trying to make conversation. However, it was not until there was a little knock on the door and Harry made his entry that they became truly animated.

Helen was seated with her back to the door and had difficulty in resisting her urge to crane her neck around, especially as she saw Isabel's blushing response to his greeting. Queen Matilda graciously invited him to take the seat to the left of Helen, which would normally be occupied by Peter.

To Helen's intense annoyance, her mother promptly took the lead in conversation from her seat at the far end of the table, making it impossible for her to look round to where Harry was now seated.

"Helen, would you do us the honour of introducing us to your charming companion, who I believe has valiantly come to your aid on several occasions. Your sister Isabel and I have only met him, under informal circumstances, so far. Considering the debt of gratitude that you owe him, it would be fitting if you could help us all to be more appropriately acquainted with this young man."

Helen felt deeply embarrassed by her mother's heavy sarcasm. Even if the poor old fellow had scrubbed off some of the dirt, he could hardly appreciate being described as young and charming.

Taking a deep breath, Helen turned to face him. She found herself staring at a handsome face, with ash-blond hair swept loosely across his forehead. The only part of him that seemed familiar were the laughing green eyes.

"Harry, is that really you?" she uttered before she had composed herself.

King Geoffrey took pity on his eldest daughter.

"Surely you remember hearing about Harry before, my dear. In his youth, he served alongside Peter at the Battle of Sapling Beech. Later on, when he was in need of employment, I was delighted to appoint him as our royal forester. It seems that this was a good appointment, given his recent service to our family in the forest."

King Geoffrey's speech had given Helen the opportunity to survey the profile of her neighbour. Of medium build, Harry had a rugged face, with high cheekbones. Now that its length had been so drastically reduced, his hair appeared thick and wavy. As the King finished speaking, Helen realised, with regret, that she had still not had enough time to recognise the Harry she thought she knew in the figure before her.

As the banquet commenced, Helen was determined not to let her previous eating eccentricities rear to the surface during the meal. She had already humiliated herself enough in this man's presence. Besides, Isabel was eating well and chatting pleasantly to Harry and Helen had no intention of being outshone by her little sister.

Swept away by his enjoyment of the evening, King Geoffrey turned to Isabel,

"My dear, why don't you delight us with one of your pretty songs. I have missed hearing you sing."

There were a few moments of silence, in which Queen Matilda glared down the table at her husband and Helen squeezed Isabel's knee reassuringly under the table.

Obediently, Isabel slowly edged her way around the table, approaching the virginal in the adjacent Hall as cautiously as if she had been hunting down a bear.

Remembering that the court musician had been dismissed after constant criticism of his playing by Aaron, Queen Matilda curtly rose to take her place at the virginal. She had still failed to catch the King's eye. Her playing sounded a little uneven. However, once Isabel started singing, the Queen's inadequacies paled into insignificance. Isabel's voice had the tone of a creaking door and the higher notes were little better than squeaks. After a single verse and chorus, Queen Matilda drew the song to an end with a flourish.

The singing was greeted with embarrassed silence and everyone concentrated on their food as Isabel and Queen Matilda hastened back to their seats. King Geoffrey said nothing but straightened his crown.

"Geoffrey, I wish you wouldn't wear that thing at mealtimes. You know you only do it to cover your bald patch."

Helen dreaded Harry making one of his sarcastic comments about the performance. When to her horror, she noticed him stop eating and sit back a little in his chair, ready to begin conversation, she desperately tugged at his sleeve. Ignoring her hint, Harry turned to Isabel.

"It was a delight to hear a lady's sweet singing again. Thank you. In the forest I do hear plenty of singing. However, the birds do not have such a fine accompanist."

Relieved that Harry had been so tactful, Helen remembered his talent for birdsong.

"I know the setting will seem rather strange but would you mind gracing us with some of your bird calls? I know that my little sister is very curious about what takes place in the forest, so I am sure she will find this very illuminating."

To the amazement of everyone but Helen and Harry, the room was suddenly filled with the sweet, clear tones of a nightingale, the trilling beauty of a blackbird and the ascending glory of a skylark.

"You sing so beautifully as a bird Harold, do you also sing as yourself?" Queen Matilda asked, once the beauty of the moment had stilled into a wistful silence.

"I'm afraid that, in my own right, I am nothing but an old crow, your Majesty" Harry laughed."However, in my heyday, I used to enjoy playing the lute."

"The lute is a strange instrument for a forester to play," Isabel commented, voicing the thoughts of her mother and sister."

At this, King Geoffrey, who had been enjoying the pleasantness of the evening, gave a chuckle.

"Oh my dear girl, you really should have learnt the lesson by now, that appearances can be deceptive."

Instead of giving further explanation, the King settled back more comfortably in his chair, much to the aggravation of the ladies in his family. Before Queen Matilda could resume the questioning, King Geoffrey announced that it was surely time for the ladies to retire.

"I should very much like to discuss the possibility of growing grapes here with our young guest."

Isabel rolled her eyes at the Queen, who simply pursed her lips at the topic of farming. Helen's agitation at sitting for so long, especially after a meal, was becoming unbearable, so she smiled gratefully at her father. By holding onto the backs of chairs, she managed to propel herself reasonably well out of the Great Hall. She had left her stick propped just outside the door and she set off hobbling remarkably quickly along the Gallery, trying to suppress the rising tide of guilt.

29

The three Princesses

Clemence, who was also engulfed by guilt, had hidden her empty plate under Beatrice's, in the hope of erasing the large quantity of food which she had consumed. She had deliberately avoided the banquet so as to keep away from the temptation of too many enticing delicacies. However, temptation had tracked her down in the form of Cook, who had prepared a large trayful of treats so that she and Beatrice did not miss out on the bounty of the banquet, which she had lovingly prepared.

Clemence wished now that she and Beatrice had gone to the banquet, as she was sure that the presence of a stranger would have curbed her appetite. To make things worse, Beatrice had fallen asleep after the unusually large meal, leaving Clemence alone with her guilt.

There was a soft knock at the door. Clemence rose swiftly to answer it before a louder knock should wake Beatrice. It was Helen.

"Clemence, would you mind coming to Isabel's room with me? She's been singing again and it was pretty awful, so she's in a terrible state. I never know what to say to her when she's like this. Isabel moaned to Mother until she retired to bed early with a headache, so now it's up to us to sort her out."

Wrapping her shawl neatly around her shoulders, Clemence was glad that Beatrice was safely asleep, as this left her free to go and help her sisters. She could barely remember the last time the three of them had met up in one of their chambers to talk. Before Aaron came, they spent most of their time in each other's company. Sometimes she had felt a bit left out, as she had often lacked the confidence to say how she truly felt.

Nevertheless, Clemence had always enjoyed been one of the three Princesses and had worked hard to include Beatrice as a fourth whenever she was staying with them. She realised again how cunningly Aaron had divided them from one another, just like the fox did with the geese in the game.

By the time that they reached Isabel, she was well on her way to unravelling the embroidered border of her sleeve.

"How could you let Father ask me to sing? You've no idea how humiliating that was, especially in front of Harry."

"For goodness sake, Isabel, stop complaining. It wasn't you at your best but it wasn't too bad. Who cares what Harry thinks anyway, after all he's only the forester."

At this, Isabel started wailing again uncontrollably. Helen, having tried her best, paced angrily up and down the room using her stick.

Clemence perched on the edge of the bed next to Isabel and started stroking her hair to calm her down.

"I'm sorry I didn't manage to attend the banquet. You see, you're so much braver than I am. Besides you'll always be a much better singer than Helen and I put together."

Isabel started to choke back her tears enough to speak.

"I'm just so frightened that I'll never have my voice back the way it was. I didn't realise how much it meant to me, until I destroyed it."

"You didn't destroy it any more than I wrecked my chances of dancing beautifully. It was Aaron who did."

"I don't care whose fault it is, I just can't bear the thought that I'll never be able to sing again." Isabel's head slumped forward.

Clemence hesitated for a few moments and then said quietly.

"Do you remember how we always used to laugh when dear old Priscilla was trying to get us to eat our supper and go to bed. She'd tell us that we needed nourishment and rest, just like the little bulbs under the ground in winter, so that we could grow into the beautiful blossoms we wanted to be in the spring."

They all started giggling at the memory of their elderly governess wagging her finger at them earnestly, night after night, as they thought of more and more elaborate excuses for not going to bed.

"Anyway, I was thinking that you, young Isabel, need to give that voice of yours proper rest and nourishment, so that it can bloom when the time is right."

By now Helen and Isabel were rocking to and fro with laughter, as Clemence expertly mimicked Priscilla's voice and mannerisms.

"I shouldn't mock, she was a kind enough old thing really. However, I do think she had a point and I really believe that your voice will come back just as beautiful as ever, as long as you give it a chance. Just think of Beatrice. Her throat was terribly swollen and painful and she could barely swallow, let alone speak. Even so, after a week or so of resting in bed and taking proper care of herself, she's showing great improvement. I think we've all been too harsh with ourselves, just like Aaron wanted us to be. I think we all need to accept that it's time to change, however hard that's going to feel."

"To be honest, Clemence, I think you hold yourself in too low a regard. What you've just said to us shows that you're an extremely brave person."

With that, Helen gave her a hug.

30

A serving of fear

The following evening, King Geoffrey was overjoyed to see all three of his daughters, along with his young granddaughter, reunited once more around the banquet table. His wife and all three daughters had warned him of the consequences of asking Isabel to sing, so tonight he was resigned to allowing the ladies to lead the conversation. However, he was surprised when it was Harry who addressed him,

"Your Majesty, please forgive me for being so presumptuous. There is, however, a matter I should very much like to discuss with you. I have noticed that the castle is considerably overgrown with ivy. As your forester, I am aware that healthy trees become damaged if ivy is allowed to smother them. I should advise you to take every opportunity to weaken the hold that this most greedy and stubborn of plants has over Great Roseindid. It will not be easy for your gardeners, since the ivy clings so fiercely to the stonework that it leaves a trail of damage behind it, even when it is removed. However, I most strongly recommend that you repel the ivy from your walls with the same determination that you would use to deter any other invading force."

At this, Queen Matilda gave a sigh. After a moment's reflection, King Geoffrey replied,

"Thank you, young man. I admire your courage and your concern for our castle's well-being. I shall take your advice and request that the matter is dealt with by the gardeners at the earliest opportunity."

After this, Harry looked far more at ease and King Geoffrey was at least able to console himself with the thought that he was being a considerate host to his forester.

All his daughters were making an effort to eat, even if this seemed slow and laboured up to their previously healthy appetites. It was a joy to have Beatrice's company again, though she looked pale and anxious at times. It was only when Helen asked her directly what the news was from her father, that it became obvious why she was so concerned. In a quiet voice, she explained,

"I'm very sorry, Auntie Helen, but I haven't got anything to tell you. Since I've been ill, Father had been sending William with a letter every day. However, for the past three days, there has been no word from him."

Queen Matilda quickly answered,

"Don't worry my dear. I'm sure your father is just too busy with matters of state to write every day. He's probably just realised that you're feeling better."

"Don't be absurd, Mother. You know as well as I do that Peter's not like that. Writing to Beatrice would be his first thought of the day, especially as she has been so poorly."

"Mother, I have to agree with Helen, it is strange. Three days ago Beatrice was still very ill. I can't believe that Peter would stop writing until he heard better news. Besides, Beatrice has been telling me that the news from the Eastern province is that the flood problems are now all under control. Peter was hoping to arrive next week for the start of his visit with us."

"Why did nobody think of telling me this before? After all, I am his mother."

Harry suddenly interrupted the conversation, much to everyone's surprise.

"Did you say that the letters stopped coming these past three days?"

Beatrice nodded. Turning to King Geoffrey, Harry said slowly and carefully,

"Your Majesty, it may be purely a coincidence but I can't help but notice that the letters have stopped arriving since I have been staying at the castle. I know that William's route took him through the forest, since he often stopped at my lodge for a rest and some ale."

Helen bridled at this.

"Given the nature of the attack which took place, I have concerns regarding William's safety. In the circumstances, I beg leave to return to my duties in the forest and I will do all that I can to discover the truth. Please forgive me for neglecting my duties."

"You can't possibly go back to your work as forester with your injuries. You know full well that you've got to rest for weeks."

Helen's cheeks were flushed and her eyes looked frightened. Memories of that terrible evening had come flooding back to haunt her.

"That's right m'boy. It's brave of you to offer but you're in no fit state to enter the fray just now. I shall send Sam tonight with a letter explaining our concerns to Peter and we'll lay these fears to rest. Please don't worry yourselves."

"Not tonight, dear. I shall draft the letter myself first thing tomorrow and Sam can take it then. I wouldn't want the young boy having to go through the forest at this time of night."

"If it pleases your Majesty, I would suggest a different route for Sam. He could travel through the village and then north of Bracken Lake. Then he would be approaching the Eastern province from the north, using the river crossing near the disused barracks. It will take a few hours longer but I strongly recommend that he avoid the forest until we know that it's safe."

31

Fear for the prince

As Sam passed the weather-beaten stonework of the old army barracks, he reflected on how glad he was that King Geoffrey, unlike his father, who had been the previous king, had been determined not to lead his country into war. Sam enjoyed his life at the castle, tending the horses and helping with chores or at least he had, until Molly died. Much of the time now, he felt as cold and empty as the barracks he was riding past.

Although apprehensive about having to take a different route, Sam was very relieved not to have to go into the forest alone again. He smiled to himself as he saw the sun rising over the small, sturdy Gorsebank Castle with its moat glistening in the morning light.

~~~~~~~~~~

Helen also paused to enjoy the beauty of the morning, which gave Harry enough time to bring his horse alongside hers. He was riding carefully, one arm still in a sling. She had asked him to keep her company for a reason, since had she did not want the others to hear what she had to say.

"I'm really sorry, Harry, but I need you to think back to the evening Aaron attacked us. I've recently remembered something he said and it's worrying me terribly. I'm hoping that you were conscious enough to have heard it too. Do you remember him saying anything about Peter?"
~~~~~~~~~~

Harry's brow furrowed with concentration. Finally he had to admit that he could remember nothing that had been said.

"Maybe, if you say what you heard, it might jog my memory."

"Well, it was after he stabbed you. He leaned over you and muttered something. I believe it was,

'So much for the protector of princesses, now for the precious. .'"

"Prince himself," interrupted Harry. "When you started saying them, I could hear the loathsome words lodged somewhere in my head."

Helen suddenly started to tremble.

"Oh Harry, I'm so sorry to have got you involved in all this and I'm so frightened about what he might have done to Peter. Maybe Aaron has already been to Gorsebank Castle and killed everyone. That would explain why Beatrice hasn't heard anything. He'd never have stopped writing to her otherwise. She's all he's got since Katherine died."

"Princess Helen, I'm sure Peter can take care of himself. He's the best swordsman I know and, from what I've heard, he easily defeated Aaron last time they met."

"Yes, but Aaron's so cunning and cruel. As he knows that Peter is the better swordsman, he'll set a trap or stab him in the back or something horrible."

Harry was unsure what to say. He was so used to Helen being self-assured to the point of arrogance. Now, here she was, white-faced and trembling.

"I'm glad you didn't speak of your fears in front of everyone. Hopefully Sam will be back this evening with good news from Prince Peter and a long letter for Princess Beatrice. The threat from Aaron remains and we will have to think up a plan to deal with him long before your brother comes riding through the forest on his way to collect his daughter. When is he due to arrive?"

"The end of next week. That hardly gives us any time."

"Please don't worry, that should be plenty of time, as long as we all work together and no one takes matters into their own hands. As for now, please dry your eyes and be brave. If Queen Matilda thinks that I've upset you, I fear that being banished would not be seen as punishment enough."

"Quite honestly, Harry, with my father on the throne, you'd probably be given some dung-shovelling to help you repent of your mischievous ways."

"I wouldn't object, though I think Prince Peter might do if he thought I was doing it in his fine velvet clothes!"

At this, Helen could not help smiling.

"We must tell Father and Mother as soon as possible, though, and I think I should break the news to Clemence and Isabel, though not to Beatrice. She's too young to be burdened with the prospect of losing her father as well as her mother."

"Don't you think it would be advisable to wait for Sam's return before sharing our worries? After all, it will only mean delaying for one day."

"Wait a day? How absurd! I'm not letting another day go by without making plans to destroy that malicious man before he does any more harm. Do you think Aaron's out there twiddling his thumbs, wasting away a whole day? I can tell you that he isn't and, what's more, I'm not going to either and, believe it or not, neither are you. We're going straight back now to tell the others all we know."

With that, Helen tugged at her horse's reins, swiftly building up speed to a gallop, whilst Harry trotted his horse carefully in her wake.

~~~~~~~~~~

As Sam crossed the drawbridge, he suddenly wondered if Prince Peter would be angry with him for bringing a complaint about his recent failure to write to his daughter. What business was it of his to insist that a Prince write a letter every day? To be honest, he hardly ever heard from his mum. Even then it was just a few words of message, which the fishmonger repeated to him when he visited the castle.

Sam was relieved to see William busy in the stables. He suddenly realised that he could ask him about the letters. Maybe William would
~~~~~~~~~~

know the answer to the mystery of the letters without him having to ask Prince Peter. He had never had cause to challenge a prince until now and it was not something he would do if he could help it. Besides, William was good company and Sam reflected that he would enjoy a chat over a glass of ale if he was asked.

William looked surprised to see him.

"Good gracious young Sam. Surely you've not brought an answer already. I've only just returned from delivering the last one. I'm fair worn out with all the letters recently. How's Princess Beatrice now? We've all been desperately worried about her. How terrible it was that she should have broken her arm like that and then to have that mysterious fever as well, poor little mite."

"What are you talking about William? Princess Beatrice has certainly suffered but her condition was due to a sore throat. It's the forester, Harry who's in a sling."

"That's strange. The new forester said he'd died in an accident. I'm glad to hear he's all right after all. Nice fellow is Harry. Mind you, the new forester is more generous with the ale and he's always got time for a sit and a chat. Lucky he is so friendly, what with the new rules from the King."

"What new rules and who are you going on about? Harry is still the forester. There's no one been appointed to look after the forest in his place. It seems as if you've been drinking your ale by the bucket!"

"No more than you by the sounds of it! You don't seem to know anything about what's going on. Spent too time shovelling manure, I reckon."

"No I haven't! Please tell me what you're going on about, William. I've come here to ask why Prince Peter has stopped writing to Princess Beatrice these last few days."

"What's wrong with you? Haven't you been listening to anything I've said. His Highness writes every evening and I'm up before dawn delivering them."

"But they don't get to Great Roseindid Castle."

"Course they do. I take them as far as the forester's lodge and he gives me a letter from Princess Helen to bring back. It was different before the family were all taken with that fever because I used to come up to the castle in person. Now the King is so worried about spreading the illness that I can go no further than the lodge in the forest."

"Oh William, this is all nonsense. The Royal family aren't suffering with any fever. The only thing that's wrong with them is that they're sick of not hearing any news from Prince Peter. As for Princess Helen writing to him, that's not true either. I don't know where those letters came from. It's poor little Princess Beatrice that's been writing and waiting for you to come and take her letters home for her."

"That thieving, lying forester! Who is he and what on earth is he playing at?"

"I don't know for sure. What I do know is that I've got to speak to the Prince and explain all of this. Perhaps he could write a little letter to put Princess Beatrice's mind at rest?"

"That's the worst of it. The message from Princess Helen asked him to come and help them as soon as possible. He set off this morning to do the final Royal visits and then he planned to come straight from them to the Castle of Great Roseindid."

"Where is he now?"

"I've no idea which places he has yet to visit. Best thing you can do is to get back to the castle as fast as you can and warn them of what's been happening. Please tell Princess Beatrice that I am truly sorry if my foolishness has caused her upset. I didn't mean any harm."

As Sam took a last deep sip of his glass of ale and started to ride back across the drawbridge, he heard William calling after him,

"Whatever you do lad, don't go through the forest."

Shaking his head and shuddering a little, Sam thought to himself that this was the last thing he was likely to do.

32

Keeping secrets

Harry perched uneasily on a chair in the Council Chamber. Isabel was sitting and stroking Cleo next to him. Helen had seated herself with her back to the dais. Clemence was curled up in the window seat, hugging her knees.

"I know what you're saying, but I feel very bad about not including Beatrice in these discussions. Peter's her father after all and I can't help feeling that she would want to be helping as much as possible."

"Oh Clemence, it's only until we hear what Sam has to say. Then I promise to let you tell Beatrice all that she needs to know. You agree with me, don't you Harry?"

At these words of Helen's, Isabel and Clemence exchanged a lingering glance.

"I certainly do agree and, personally, I'm not sure how much the royal rat is contributing to our plan."

"Don't tease Isabel, she'll start screaming and then she'll tell Mother everything."

"You ignorant savage! This is a guinea pig, I'll have you know. Kindly remember that. Cleo is more entitled to be here than you. She lives here and you're only a guest."

By now, Isabel was stroking the guinea pig so fervently that that they were both covered in a haze of white hair.

"Don't you think we should get back to the reason why we're here in the first place? Does anyone have any ideas for protecting Peter from Aaron?"snapped Helen.

"The main thing is to warn him that there may be a threat. Once Sam has returned and had a good night's sleep, we should send him back to warn Prince Peter that on no account is he to travel through the forest on his way here. I also suggest that he rides here in the company of William. He isn't the most fearsome of fighters but there is always safety in numbers."

"But I hate the thought of that man lying in wait for my brother and us having no idea where he is and what his plans are. I know the last time I went into the forest was a disaster but I'd rather go out and look for him than just wait here, allowing him to attack just as he likes."

"No, Helen, for once you've got to be patient. It's like that game Fox and Geese. When we're all here together, we're safe from his attack. It's only if we end up wandering round on our own that he can pick us off. We should get Peter safely here first and then worry about what to do next."

~~~~~~~~~~~

The banquet that evening was more subdued than that of the previous evenings'. Beatrice sensed that she was being left out of something important and this, coupled with another day of no letter from her father, made her feel wretchedly isolated and homesick.

King Geoffrey wondered if he had said something tactless the previous evening but could bring nothing to mind. Queen Matilda sensed the air of anxiety but could think of nothing to account for it, so felt rather irritable. She decided that she might press upon the subject later with Isabel.

Harry broke the silence by asking King Geoffrey about the nation's defences since the end of the War of Ten New Moons. There was a long pause. Then King Geoffrey said wearily,
~~~~~~~~~~~

"You know my boy, I am not by nature a military man, unlike my father and my two dear brothers, both of whom were killed during the previous war that my father waged against the Renetians, when I was just a young lad. I have no hankerings after other men's lands. This kingdom is a good place which gives us everything we could possibly need. However, our simple harvests and resources are not noteworthy enough to attract the envy of others. There is no reason we should not all live at peace."

"Oh Geoffrey, you know full well that that assumes that all men are as good and peace-loving as you. Believe me, they are not!"

At that moment Amy appeared breathless at the door of the Great Hall.

"Begging your pardon, your Majesty, but Sam has just returned and I think you should hear his news as soon as possible."

King Geoffrey adjusted his crown and rose to his feet.

"Where are you going Geoffrey? Everyone here wants to know, and has a right to know, what Sam has to say. Please show him in immediately, Amy."

At this, the King slumped back into his chair, muttering something about only trying to protect the ladies.

Sam wiped the sweat from his brow before entering the Great Hall. Initially tongue-tied, Helen's questions soon helped him to explain all that he had learned from William.

"But what does this pretend forester look like?"

"I'm so sorry, Princess Isabel. I didn't think to ask."

Silence fell for a moment and then Helen retorted.

"Don't be ridiculous Isabel, we all know perfectly well who it is."

33

The forest by lamplight

Clemence was relieved that Beatrice had made her excuses to leave the banquet and go to bed early. It meant that she would be able to join the others in the Council Chamber as soon as possible to decide what should be done. It was going to require much skill to calm Helen down, now she realised that Aaron had been forging her handwriting in order to trick Peter into danger. The King and Queen were baffled by this strange behaviour on the part of the former tutor. However, without the knowledge that he wanted to kill Peter, Sam's information seemed less deadly.

~~~~~~~~~~~~

"But we have to act tonight. We've no idea when Peter will be travelling this way but Aaron may well know precisely what his movements will be. It's maddening!"

"Princess Helen, if it might be permitted, I should like to borrow Prince Peter's riding cloak and the horse he would usually ride when he is here. In this way, I might be able to fool Aaron into believing that I am the Prince. I could take the long route round past the village and approach the forest from the Eastern Province."

"And get killed for your trouble. You'll have no more protection from Aaron's merciless hatred than Peter would. It just won't work and don't you dare scream, Isabel."

Out of the corner of her eye, Helen had seen her youngest sister breathing more and more rapidly and twitching her hands about.
~~~~~~~~~~~~

To everyone's surprise Clemence swiftly interrupted,

"Stop squabbling. I have a plan but it's vital that we work together as a team. Just like the geese in the game, we must work together to outwit the fox and protect one another. Thinking about Aaron, the only sort of person who is going to lure him out of his hiding place, without him immediately attacking them, is a princess. Just like when you found him, Helen, he'll be like a cat tormenting a mouse. So we three are his bait. I just wish there were more of us."

Suddenly there was movement in the inglenook fireplace and a figure wrapped in a full length black riding cape stepped out and pulled back the hood.

"Auntie Clemence, there are more, trust me."

~~~~~~~~~~~

Two hours later, Amy was sitting opposite Cook and mechanically stroking Cleo, who had been handed to her by Isabel.

"You do realise that you'll have to hold her instead if the King or Queen ring for me."

Cook grimaced, as she replied, ed slightly and gave a sigh.

"I can't believe that tonight of all nights we're stuck here looking after a guinea pig."

"You know as well as I do that this is the only way that Clemence could get Isabel to take part and it seems that she's very important to the plan."

"I really don't like all these secrets. I've never hidden anything from the King or Queen before and I wish we didn't have to today. Besides, what will happen if it goes wrong? How can we possibly explain this to their Majesties if anything bad happens to one of their children?"

"But they're not children any more. . . only Beatrice and even she is growing up fast. They know what they're doing. We've just got to trust them."

~~~~~~~~~~~

It had taken a surprisingly long time for Helen to get into place near the forester's lodge. It had been hard for her not to cry out with the pain in her ankle but she knew how important it was to keep the plot a surprise until everyone was ready.

Sam had supported her, though he was stumbling himself over the long hem of Isabel's dress. When told she had to provide a disguise for the stable boy, Isabel had at first been angry, until she remembered the dress with the frayed cuffs. Maybe, in these circumstances, Mother would allow her to have a new one.

Helen had found the idea of dressing Harry as herself very amusing, especially as Harry was so indignant. She had carefully chosen the most frilly, pink gown in her wardrobe for him, with a matching pink lace shawl to mask his injured arm and rose-trimmed headdress to cover his ash blonde hair. Sam was relieved that Isabel provided a hooded cape instead.

Having to stay still in one place, waiting for the attack to begin, was agonising for Helen. Suddenly she heard the nightingale call start, stop and start again. Harry and Isabel must be in place. She had to act now. Drawing in a deep breath, she shouted,

"Isabel, come back, I can't keep up with you. You must listen to me for once, Aaron doesn't want to see you, he'll only hurt you."

When they heard Aaron open the lodge door, Helen and Sam, carrying a metal lantern between them, headed as fast as they could towards the clearing. In the thicket, they silently handed the lantern to Harry and Isabel, themselves slipping away for a few yards into the shadows and hiding behind bushes.

Isabel ran a little ahead of a limping Harry, who was carrying the lantern. They passed through the clearing, opening the door of the lantern so that the candle's full brightness illuminated them. By now they could hear Aaron stealthily prowling after them.

At the far side of the clearing they dimmed the lamp, by shutting its door, so that only chinks of lamplight could creep through the slits in the metal. They ran together as fast as they could to the steps of the Mausoleum. Harry turned to Isabel and whispered,

"Go for it!"

At that she gave a scream that could curdle milk.

"Practice makes perfect", she whispered back, as they handed the lamp to Clemence, who had been hiding by the Mausoleum. They then squirreled themselves into the undergrowth to hide. Harry held Isabel's hand as they crouched together motionless, until Aaron had passed. They could hear his measured breathing perfectly in time with his relentless footsteps following them along the path.

Clemence took a deep breath. This was the moment she had been dreading. In the loudest voice that she could muster, slightly choked with emotion, she called out,

"Beatrice, I'm so sorry. I've got to leave you. Isabel must be in terrible trouble. I've got to go and help her. You'll be safe if you stay here in the Mausoleum. Look, I've unlocked the door for you. I'll be back as soon as I can."

Giving Beatrice's hand a squeeze, Clemence ran off with the lantern, back to where the others were hiding, just in case Aaron preferred to follow her. However, she knew in her heart that he would never be able to resist the chance of terrifying Beatrice in the imprisoning tomb. It would be the perfect way for him to exact revenge on her for getting him banished from the kingdom.

Beatrice's heart was pounding so loudly in her ears that it was impossible for her to hear whether other feet were following her into the cold, damp stone building. There she swiftly pulled back the tapestry, revealing a low, dark tunnel, just as Clemence had described it.

Hunching herself over, she was able to run through the darkness, her footfalls leaving an eerie echo. She was glad that Aaron was so tall. He would have to go on all fours to fit through the passage. She knew that Sam, Isabel and Clemence would be following Aaron along the tunnel as fast as they could go, with Sam leading in case he turned and attacked them. Neither Helen nor Harry would be able to manage crawling along because of their injuries. They would be collecting the horse from where it had been tethered, just inside the forest and then riding back to the castle in order to await their arrival.

~~~~~~~~~~~

Before Harry could help Helen get up from the undergrowth, a gauntleted hand clutched his arm. A tall dark figure had appeared behind him.

"Helen, I can't believe you are out here at this time of night. You could at least have the decency to look at me when I'm talking to you."

At that, Harry slowly turned round, his embarrassment framed with pink frills.

"Harry, what on earth are you doing in Helen's clothes? I asked you to look after her, not impersonate her!"

There was a rustling nearby and Helen emerged,

"That's typical of you, Peter. Here we are trying to save you and you ride in on your high horse. By the way, where is your horse?"

"Helen, what's wrong with you? You know what you asked me to do in your last letter. You told me to dismount at the lodge on my way to Great Roseindid in order to pick up some of Harry's belongings from the new forester. Besides, what do you mean about trying to save me? I'm here early because of Beatrice's illness. How is she?"

~~~~~~~~~~~

Beatrice was panting and she had a painful stitch in her side. After what seemed like forever, she could now see a light ahead. She knew that she would soon be inside the castle. She was so glad that Harry and Helen were going to get there first to rescue her from Aaron.

Beatrice could hear Aaron closing in on her, advancing in leaps and bounds, his fingernails clawing against the stonework. As the passage came to an end, it narrowed as it sloped upwards. Beatrice had to fall to her hands and knees to clamber the last few yards. Terror got the better of her and she let out a piercing scream, which ricocheted along the tunnel and into the depths of the castle.

As Beatrice emerged into the dungeon, she choked on the stagnant air. Looking wildly around her for her rescuers, she could see no sign of either Harry or Helen. For a moment she was alone.

All too soon, Beatrice could hear Aaron slithering through the opening to the tunnel. Too terrified to look around, she cradled herself into a ball. Behind her she could hear feet pounding on the stone steps and then a loud thud. Then another, as a voice behind her shouted.

"And that one's for Molly!"

Beatrice was still frozen in fear until she heard Amy's voice beside her and felt an arm around her shoulders.

"You're safe now, Beatrice. No one can harm you."

Turning slowly around, Beatrice saw Cook still standing over the collapsed form of Aaron, brandishing her rolling pin.

34

Appointment of a Royal Guard

Everyone was gathered around the table apart from Harry. He and Peter had been taking it in turns to guard Aaron in the dungeon, although Harry had insisted that Peter take the first watch so that he had time to change into another set of borrowed clothes. This time they were Peter's.

"What puzzles me is how you came to know about the tunnel from the castle?"

"Well, Father, there has to be some compensation for spending months locking myself away in the dungeon. I grew sick of the ivy poking its way in everywhere, so I started pulling it out. In one corner the stonework was completely curtained with it. When I tugged hard, some of the stones came away with the ivy, revealing the entrance to the passageway. Feeling that the dark path could offer no more terrors than those already plaguing my mind, I pressed forward until I emerged in a strange building decorated with stained glass. I later realised that it was the Mausoleum. It may sound a bit strange, but to me it became a place of refuge. On the evening that Aaron attacked Harry, I went to the kitchen but there was no food that I wanted. I was so angry that on my way back I put the key to the Mausoleum in my pocket. I had no idea then how useful it was going to be."

Eventually, Peter's voice cut through the silence.

"I've just remembered some important news that I heard during my visit to our border with Renetia. Aaron is a wanted man there. Apparently, he slaughtered two courtiers in his attempt to abduct their young princess. Since he had already been banished from Great Roseindid, I didn't expect to find him here, so advised them to search elsewhere, which I now regret. I hadn't realised how badly he wanted revenge. In the circumstances, I feel that I should return as soon as possible, visiting the Renetian Court on the way. I'm sure they will be only too glad to take charge of our prisoner."

"Oh Peter, surely you don't need to leave again so soon?"

"It is important, Mother. Besides, if Beatrice and I leave now, I think we could allow ourselves a month here around Christmas and New Year. Does that suit you, Beatrice?"

"Yes, Father, just as long as Grandma and Grandad promise not to hire any more tutors in the meantime."

~~~~~~~~~~~

As the early morning mist melted into radiant sunshine, the gilded royal carriage made its way towards Renetia. Beatrice was bubbling over with excitement at the prospect of seeing Bright and Mabel on their return home. Underneath this rising joy was a sense of peace that, however much she grew and changed during this coming year, the aunties she was leaving behind would be there for her next year.

When the carriage finally faded from view, Harry turned to Helen,

"It was kind of Sam and Cook to take a turn at guarding Aaron, so that I could make my farewells to Prince Peter and Princess Beatrice. I suppose that, when Aaron has been taken away, I shall return to the forest. I'm almost fully recovered and I imagine that the greatest danger that lurks in the forest now is that of trees falling over from neglect."

Harry was surprised and startled when he noticed Helen swiftly brushing away tears from her eyes. King Geoffrey cleared his throat.
~~~~~~~~~~~

"Peter and I had a talk this morning and we have decided that we need a Royal Guard. I was wondering whether you might accept the post."

Queen Matilda threaded her arm through his and said quietly,

"Well done, Geoffrey. That is a very wise move."

"I am truly honoured your Majesty, though Cook proved to be a somewhat better guard than I did."

"None of us would ever underestimate the fearsome power of her rolling pin. However, it would be good if she were free to use it preparing pastry and scones, both of which she does beautifully. We have great faith in your abilities, Harry."

"Besides," Helen interrupted. "I've noticed a fair few tree roots intruding into the castle grounds. I don't want to find myself tripping up."

A broad grin spread across Harry's face, giving them all the answer they had been hoping for.

May all those who after this book found
That their heads were just as ivy-wound,
Find what the princesses came to know...
And end their Great Roseindid's woe